GIRLS' LIFE MAGAZINE

GL *The Girls' Life*
BIG BOOK
of FRIENDSHIP FICTION

Edited by
Lizzie Skurnick

Illustrated by
Lisa Parett

Scholastic Inc.
New York • Toronto • London • Auckland • Sydney
Mexico City • New Delhi • Hong Kong • Buenos Aires

ISBN: 0-439-44985-5

12 11 10 9 8 7 6 5 4 3 2 1   4 5 6 7 8 9/0

Printed in the U.S.A.

First Scholastic printing, July 2004

Contents

Read-o-rama!

What's more important in life than friendship? Absolutely, positively nothing—and that's why this entire *GL* book of short stories is dedicated to the theme! This isn't just a book about buddy-buddy bliss, though—these stories show friendship in all its crazy flavors, sizes, styles, and colors.

As you know, your relationship with your buds and BFFs can roller-coast from thrilling highs to stomach-churning loop-de-loops. In this book, we've tried to show the entire friendship ride.

So, why are our friends so important to us? Well, maybe because they know our deepest, darkest secrets, and if we don't keep those people happy—they're sure to blab! *Just kidding*! But likely, it's because they're like family...only better, because they're family we've picked ourselves.

So pull up under a tree, grab your best bud, and start reading! You might find someone familiar inside—YOU!

Karen

Karen Bokram
Editor-in-Chief, *GL*

Spores and Bores

Leslie Margolis

*Sage might be the weirdest girl Allison has ever met.
So why does Allison like hanging out with her better than her
two best friends, Olivia and Steph?*

Sage isn't a name—it's an herb. At least that's what Olivia says about my new lab partner. We call her "Herb," but it's not like we're mean about it. We only say it behind her back when we know she's not listening. Anyway, if she *did* hear us, I'm *so* sure she wouldn't care. Herb has stood out since day one at Albert Einstein Middle School. The rest of us came into the sixth grade from one of four elementary schools around Cleveland. Herb says she comes from Boston. I would've guessed Mars.

It's not just the way she looks. Her hair is pale and straight, like dried wheat grass. She's constantly pushing her bangs out of her pointy face and her eyes remind me of black, shiny marbles. And it's not just how she dresses, in baggy patchwork dresses, black and white striped tights, and purple combat boots.

It's also how she acts. Whenever she's not in class—when, say, she's eating lunch, walking through the halls, waiting for the bus, or whatever—she wears these clunky headphones over her ears. She doesn't even take them off to eat, which she does alone. After she finishes her food, she drums on her notebook. Her fingers fly so fast they blur, so you have to look twice to make sure she's not actually using sticks. Sometimes, her lips move, like she's singing along to the music, but no sound ever comes out.

So, of course I didn't choose to be Herb's lab partner, especially not for something as important as this Saturday's science fair. Not when things were working out great with my old partners, Olivia and Steph.

For our experiment, we were observing plants, growing four ferns under the same light, but using different substances to water them: Tap water, Evian, Orange Vitamin Water, and Diet Dr. Pepper. Olivia's sister, Samira, did the same experiment five years ago, except she used Lime Gatorade instead of Orange Vitamin Water. We figured that Gatorade and Vitamin Water would have the same effects on a plant, since they're both funny-colored, processed versions of water. So all we had to do was change a few words, and we'd be set.

Things were under control, so it only seemed normal to put our feet up on our desks and catch up on all the latest gossip after we finished feeding the plants. I don't know why our teacher, Mr. Harrison, totally overreacted. First, he just yelled. Then he said that one of us would have to switch groups. Olivia and Steph volunteered me, right away. I can't say I blame them. They've been best friends forever. They only started talking to me about two months ago.

Anyway, that's how I got stuck with Herb. She's growing mold spores on organic pita bread. First, she exposed four pieces of bread to the air for different amounts of time: Fifteen minutes, thirty minutes, forty-five minutes, and one hour. Then she sealed each piece in a plastic bag. The mold started growing overnight. Disgusting, huh?

I'm supposed to be writing my observations down right now, but how much is there to say about mold? It's blue-ish gray and it looks, well, moldy. Done. Class is almost over so I'm outta here.

Lab Notes, Tuesday

Get this. Yesterday, Herb stayed after school to work on our experiment 'cause she said I didn't observe well. She actually measured the mold and weighed each slice of bread. Everyone else just goes through the motions, doing work because they have to. Herb actually seems to like it. What a freak!

Something else about Herb I noticed today. Suddenly, her ears have a lot more metal in them than they used to. Turns out, last night she got her ears triple pierced. "Wasn't that so painful?" I had to ask. The only earrings I wear are clip-ons. I was supposed to get my ears pierced last year, but I get squeamish around needles, and I chickened out. I could never admit this to Olivia and Steph. When they asked me why I didn't pierce my ears like every other cool sixth grader, I told them that my mom was really strict and she was making me wait until high school. Luckily, they bought it.

Anyway, Herb said it hardly hurt.

"Wasn't it freaky seeing that big metal gun so close to your brain?" I wondered.

"Not so much," Sage replied, looking at me like I was the crazy one.

"I'd totally pierce my ears," I told her. "But my mom won't let me until I'm in high school."

I didn't feel bad lying to Herb about this. Since I didn't tell my friends the truth, there's no way I'd tell it to *her*.

Herb said, "Why do you need permission? They're *your* ears."

"I guess," I shrugged, not knowing what else to say.

"My mom said no way could I even *think* about getting my ears double pierced. So instead, I went to the mall and got them triple pierced."

I stifled a laugh because Mr. Harrison was watching. He wasn't the only one, either. Olivia whipped her head around and rolled her eyes at me. I smirked right back at her. Herb pretended not to notice, but I could tell she did. Now she's measuring the stupid mold, and I'd better help her.

Lab Notes, Wednesday

It's amazing how quickly this mold grows. Today, it's a deeper shade of blue, and the moldiest piece looks like a baby swamp-creature. Not that it matters, but I'd much rather concentrate on science than think about yesterday. Steph and Olivia totally surprised me by riding their bikes over to my place after school. I was shooting hoops in the driveway with Jeff and Chris, my older twin brothers.

I asked Steph and Olivia if they wanted to play ball with us. Steph, who never answers for herself, looked at Olivia, and Olivia was all, "I don't want to mess up my nails." So, then I asked them if they wanted to go inside, and Olivia goes, "No, we'll just sit here and watch." And she plopped herself down on the grass. Of course, Steph did the same.

Except I knew they weren't really interested in basketball. All they wanted to do was gawk at my brothers, Jeff and Chris.

This isn't the first time this sort of thing has happened. Everyone in my family looks kind of alike because we're all tall and we have dark hair and green eyes. But my brothers are identical twins, and a lot of girls think they're cute. They get lots of attention, especially lately, since they're actually in a Doublemint Gum commercial. They filmed it last summer and it just started airing on TV two months ago. These days, it's impossible to watch my favorite shows without catching Jeff and Chris jumping hurdles in tandem, playing doubles tennis with some pretty girl twins, and then folding gum into their mouths and flashing goofy smiles at the camera.

Last week, when we were in line at the movies, this girl walked over to them and actually asked for their autographs. Being small-town celebrities kind of freaks my brothers out, but we've come to expect the weird behavior from strangers. However, having my friends act that way was a different story. I could tell Jeff and Chris were annoyed with me, but what could I do?

It was bad enough when Olivia and Steph were just

staring and whispering to each other, but then they started singing the Doublemint Gum commercial: "Double your pleasure, double your fun, double the—" except that's as far as they got before falling all over each other and laughing like maniacs.

A minute later, Jeff and Chris got so fed up they went inside. I turned to Olivia and Steph and asked them what they wanted to do. Olivia said, "Follow the twins."

I shook my head and answered, "Not a chance."

Olivia was like, "I should get home, anyway." She acted all sulky, like I'd done something wrong. And as usual, Steph did the same. Then they left, without even saying goodbye.

I used to think it was just a coincidence that Olivia and Steph started talking to me just a few days after my brothers' commercial started airing. Now, I'm starting to wonder....

Lab Notes, Thursday

This morning, Olivia said that Herb was moldy. That the only reason she wanted to do the pita bread experiment was so she'd cover up her smell. It was really mean and totally unfair. I thought maybe she'd realize Sage is kind of cool if I told her the story about her triple pierced ears. But when I finished, Olivia glared at me and said, "Allison Green, you are so gullible."

"What do you mean?" I asked.

Olivia was all, "You have to be eighteen to get your ears pierced without parental supervision. There's no way they would have done it to her without her mom or some other adult."

"Maybe she did it on her own, like with a thumbtack." Even as I said this, I knew it was doubtful.

"Nuh-uh," said Olivia. "You know she didn't because they look even, and they're not infected or anything."

"She's totally lying," Steph said. "Right, Olivia?"

As soon as I got to science class, I marched right up to Sage and asked, "If you didn't go with your mom to get your ears pierced, who took you?"

"My brother, Miguel," she replied.

I narrowed my eyes and asked, "How old is he?" My brother Jeff told me that you could always tell when someone is lying because when they speak, their nose moves a tiny bit to the right.

Sage stood perfectly still, her black eyes staring straight into my green ones. "Nineteen. He doesn't live with us anymore, but he was visiting."

"From where?"

"Boston. He goes to music school there."

"Does he play the drums?" I wondered.

"No, I play the drums. Miguel is all about the jazz guitar. We used to jam together."

"Huh. That's kind of cool." I know I'm supposed to be mad at Sage for having to work with her on the stupid mold project, but I was only being honest.

Since I felt bad about Olivia and Steph calling her smelly, I helped Sage weigh the bread. Each slice was about two ounces lighter. Turns out that when mold grows, it attaches to a food and actually eats it to survive. Kinda cool.

Lab Notes, Friday

I told Olivia and Steph to lay off Sage but they wouldn't. They marched up to her during lunch today and Olivia said, "Those headphones are so big, they make you look like a bug."

Of course, Sage didn't hear her because she was listening to music. I tried getting them to leave her alone, but Olivia yanked the headphones off her head, and yelled, "Hey, bug-girl! I said those headphones are too big."

Sage looked up at her, all calm, and replied, "Yes, but the sound quality is great."

I'd never seen anyone stand up to Olivia like that before, and it was impressive. At first, Olivia seemed as surprised as the rest of us. Five seconds later, she threw the headphones to the ground, grabbed Steph's hand, and pulled her away.

They left me stranded there. So, I picked up the headphones and handed them to Sage. "Sorry," I said, even though—technically—I hadn't done anything wrong.

Sage just slipped the headphones back over her ears and turned her back on me.

Now here I am in science, watching the mold. Sage still won't talk to me. She's just writing up the lab with her head tilted down, and her hair is covering her face so I can't even see anything but her pointy little chin.

"Let me help," I insisted. "We're supposed to do this together."

"That's okay," said Sage. "I'll just finish it tonight."

"Maybe I can come over after school and help," I said.

Before Sage had a chance to answer me, Olivia walked over. Totally ignoring that we were in the middle of talking, she was all, "Steph and I are gonna come over later. Okay, Allison?"

She didn't even ask me. She just, like, assumed I had nothing better to do. Normally I'd let it go, but after Tuesday night's scene, I had to ask, "Are you coming to see *me* or to see my brothers? Because Jeff and Chris aren't going to be home."

Olivia was silent.

"So you probably don't want to come over anymore, right?" I asked.

"Um," she said, glancing back at Steph. "Maybe another night would be better. I forgot that I have to help my mom with something." Then she headed back toward her plants.

It was too much. No way could I let it slide.

"Hey, Olivia," I called. "How about if you don't come by, like, ever?"

"What are you talking about?" Olivia asked, as she turned back toward me.

"If you want to hang out with me, that's cool. But don't pretend like you do, just so you can see my brothers."

I could tell by the stunned look on her face that Olivia didn't know what to say. So rather than answer me, she just walked away, shaking her head and mumbling under her breath.

As I laughed to myself, Sage raised her eyebrows at me. "What was that about?" she asked.

"I'll explain later," I promised. I was going to, too. And that wasn't all. Leaning in, I lowered my voice to a whisper. "Hey, Sage. You know how I said I couldn't pierce my ears because my mom wouldn't give me permission?"

Sage grinned. "What about it?"

"I sort of... lied. The truth is, I'm scared of the gun."

Sage turned back to the bread. "Yeah," she said, placing the moldiest piece on the scale. "I sort of figured."

She looked up at me, and we both smiled. That's when I knew I had made a *real* friend.

Saga of a Free-Throwing Angel

S.K. DUNN

Katie knows she's getting too old to dress up for Halloween.
But that doesn't mean she's ready to take on center court alone.

Rachel, Mary, and I were late to our last basketball practice because we had been totally engrossed in trying to come up with the perfect Halloween costumes—and we had come up with nada. The rest of the team was already sitting in a circle around the big net of basketballs on the gym floor doing stretches when we got there. Coach McKenna looked up from her clipboard and said, "Girls, you're late."

"It's not our fault. Katie-Skatie lost one of her shoes," Rachel said, calling me the nickname that she and Mary have called me since we were little.

"But after some detective work, we found it," Rachel added.

Coach McKenna shook her head in exasperation. "Okay, well, now that Charlie's Angels have arrived, we can begin."

And *ta-da*! There it was—right under our noses the whole time! The perfect costumes for the perfect group of three best friends on their last Halloween of all time! It made total sense! See, the three of us had been together for every Halloween since we were super-little kids. In the first picture of us together, Rachel is crying and Mary has a pacifier in her mouth. I'm smiling and happy, but you can totally see my blankie sticking out of my candy bag! Since we would be in middle school next year, our parents all seemed to have the same rule—this would be our last year to go out trick-or-treating.

"Teenagers are too old to go door to door asking for candy," Mary's mom had said. And then my mom agreed, saying she sounded right. Despite Rachel's best efforts to keep this philosophy from her own mother, eventually she did get wind of the theory (Rachel's mom travels a lot for work, but she always stays up-to-date on anything concerning her daughter) and issued the same decree for Rachel. Seemed lame, but what could we do? We were determined to make this last year a really big one—with the best costumes, the most candy, the whole bit.

After practice, the team went out for pizza because it was our last practice of the season. It was kind of weird, because, aside from this being our last year of trick-or-treating, it was also our last year of basketball. This was fine with Rachel and Mary. Rachel wasn't very good at it, and her parents had already agreed to let her try out for lacrosse in the spring. Mary was pretty good, but, as she said, "It's kind of boring...and *so* loud."

I, however, loved every heart-thumping minute of it. It had been really hard for me at first, but I had worked secretly on weekends and sometimes even after dinner to get good. I'd never told anybody—not even my BFFs—about the extra practice sessions with my dad, or the early morning runs with my mom.

The three of us were down at the end of the big pizza parlor table, making plans for our cool costumes. It was pretty easy to come up with ideas—we'd seen both *Charlie's Angels* movies four times each in the theater and, like a zillion times, on DVD. We were totally psyched to dress up like the beautiful and smart detectives who kicked butt! There was no question who would be which Angel—Rachel was the obvious Alex because she's the serious one (and her mom's Japanese), Mary was totally Natalie, complete with the dancing booty-thing. That left me as Dylan, which was fine, because I think she's the coolest one, anyway.

But right after we ordered, Mary started to complain. "What about 'Three Blind Mice'? I thought we were going as 'Three Blind Mice.' Halloween is next Friday! I already have a cane." Mary likes things to be straightforward, always according to the plan and by the rules. You can always count on her to be on time, to always have directions and the address of wherever you're going—and to always remember to say thank you to whoever's mom is driving.

Rachel, on the other hand, is always looking to the future—only not in a methodical, write-it-all-down way, but in a dreaming-of-the-future way. She calls it a "strategic dreaming toward destiny." Rach is very big on having a *destiny*, "a path to greatness," she calls it. She saw it on some show about this lady who made a million bucks selling pies from her kitchen or something. "Strategic dreaming toward destiny" practically became her mantra. She wants to be a Hollywood agent. Really!

"Look," Rachel said, "this is our last year to go trick-or-treating. Next year, it will be parties or nothing at all. And besides, 'Three Blind Mice' is a little babyish, Mary."

And that was the end of the costume discussion. Our last—and BIGGEST—Halloween of all time was in the works. And this night had all the makings for the best night of our lives. What could be a better combination than BFFs and unlimited, free candy?

We spent the next day at the mall getting stuff for our costumes.

When I got home, Coach McKenna called. "Kaitlin, exciting news. You've been invited to try out for the select team."

I got the same feeling that I get in a game when it's my turn to make a free throw. I couldn't think of anything to say, so I just said, "Really?"

She chuckled over the line. "Yes, really."

I thought about it for a second. "Just me?"

"Well, there will be other girls from other teams around the area," she said. "But from our team, it's just you."

"Are you sure?" I asked, hoping she had just misread her clipboard or something. "Nobody else from this team?"

Coach McKenna was just as decisive as she was when she was running us through our drills. "Just *you*, Kaitlin," she said.

It should have been the happiest moment of my life. Instead, I felt bad. I mean, yeah, Rachel and Mary couldn't wait for basketball to be over, and they didn't even want to play next year. But still, I'd never even been on a team without them. What if it wasn't the same? How much fun could I have playing ball with a bunch of strange girls?

And how could I possibly face tryouts without my BFFs?

"Can I think about it and let you know?" I asked.

When she answered, Coach McKenna sounded totally shocked. "What's the matter, Kaitlin? You've worked really hard this season—you deserve this!"

I felt kind of depressed. "Yeah, I know."

"Do you know that most of the girls who play on the select team play on the varsity team in high school?" Coach McKenna added. She sounded like Rachel and her strategic destiny stuff!

"I guess," I said. Whatever she said, it still didn't feel right.

She was quiet for a minute. "Is this about Mary and Rachel?"

"Can't they try out, too?" I burst out. I knew it sounded kind of pathetic, but I figured it was worth a shot.

"Look, I know they're your friends—" she began.

"My *best* friends!" I cut in.

"OK, your *best* friends," Coach McKenna allowed. Her voice got stern. "But they'll be happy for you. They'll understand."

Maybe she was right.

"Yeah, okay," I said. I'd have to see.

"Great. Be at the gym at 5:30 next Friday. And don't be late."

My mom was super-excited when I told her about the tryouts. "What an honor!" she said. She's big on getting "honors" and makes a huge deal out of any kind of prize I win—even when I sold the most magazines at school during a fund drive, once. "Wait till you tell Dad!" she exclaimed.

"Tell me what?" my dad asked, walking through the door.

"I get to try out for the select team!" I said. With him, I didn't have to hide my excitement.

Dad gave me a high 5, and then swung his hand around to give me a low 5 behind his back.

My mom said, "Let's go out to Sal's for dinner to celebrate."

"Oh no," my dad said, all serious. "She's in training."

As into honors and awards as my mom is, my dad is all about getting things done. "And make sure you write it on the calendar, so we don't forget," he said, referring to the huge calendar we started to keep in the kitchen a few years back to keep track of everybody's activities. Between my mom's garden club meetings, my basketball practices and piano lessons, and my dad's rugby games (a little embarrassing that he still plays, but he likes it), it seemed like we all had something to do every day. The calendar was our only salvation.

It was easy to spot the date for tryouts, because it was the only square colored in orange, with a sticker of a flying witch. I began to write in smallish letters around the end of the witch's broom, "Tryouts. 5:30."

But wait! Next Friday was not only Halloween....it was my *last* Halloween!

How was I going to tell Rachel and Mary that they'd be less one Angel on the last Halloween of our lives?

The next day, when Rachel and Mary came over, they stood at the bottom of the stairs and did some "karate" moves, which was actually just them flailing their arms around and kicking into the air in a crazy way. Then, they suddenly froze like the movie poster. It was so funny, I couldn't help but laugh, which made them laugh and break the pose.

Then, my mom came around the corner and said in a deep voice, "Hello, Angels."

And, of course, we three said all together, "Char-lieee!"

It was a great moment...until I remembered my other "great news." I plunked down on the stairs. "I gotta talk to you guys."

I explained the situation to them, about how Coach McKenna had called yesterday and asked me to try out for the select team. To delay the final punchline, I even revealed to them what they hadn't known before—that my dad had made a training program for me.

I must have been rambling a little too long because Mary finally interrupted and said, "So why do you seem so bummed about this, if it's what you want?"

Rachel added, "Yeah, it seems like a good thing."

I sucked in my breath and then told them. "Tryouts are Friday night. Halloween."

We all sat there for a minute, while the news kind of sunk in—and it slowly dawned on Rachel and Mary that two Angels not only wouldn't really make any sense, it might even seem weird.

I, of course, had been thinking about nothing else for the past 24 hours. Finally, I said what I had been thinking all day. "Maybe I won't go. I mean, I might not even make the stupid team. And even if I did, I won't even know anybody. What fun is that?" I asked.

Mary said, "You *have* to go. This may be your, your—" She turned to Rachel. "What're you always saying?"

"Destiny," Rachel said. "It's true. This could be the next step on the path to your destiny. Who knows—maybe you're destined to play professional basketball. And you'll never know unless you try."

So it was tryouts 1, Halloween 2, no matter what else I said.

That week, my dad went into coaching overdrive. He had me practice free throws and lay-ups, and made me do short sprints on the driveway, where he'd measured out exactly 25 yards—the official length of half of the court. He marked it up with red and blue chalk. (Well, really pink, because we couldn't find red.) It was fun, and I was glad to have the practice and spend time with him, but even I could tell it was getting a little out of hand. Still, it was good to get me ready for what I had to do on Friday... and to keep my mind off what I would be missing on Friday.

When it was time to leave for the tryouts, a group of little kids were already out in the neighborhood trick-or-treating. Some moms were pushing strollers and carrying little "bunnies." An adult was dressed as a cat, leading Three Blind Mice. That made me think of the year that Rachel, Mary, and I went as Three Men in a Tub, and how my dad had pulled us around in a boat he made from a wagon. It made me think we should have been together this year. It made me think how everything was changing, and how maybe we wouldn't be together as much anymore. It made me bummed that I wouldn't get any candy...but not as much as what I would really be missing. And the Three Blind Mice looked like a cute idea after all— even if it *was* kind of babyish.

Some girls were already at the gym when I got there, running drills and practicing lay-ups. It was totally weird to see a bunch of strange girls in our gym, and nobody, nil, nada—not a single person that I knew. That made me really nervous. I mean, when I played on our regular team, it sort of didn't matter if I messed up because we'd all played together since we were way little. But this group! Some of them looked like they were much younger and some looked much older. How could we all be the same age?

I gave my bag to my dad and walked over to Coach McKenna. I sucked in my breath a little and tried to stand up tall. That, sadly, did not make me feel any better—especially because the girl closest to me was, like, super tall—there's no way she was in sixth grade, too!

Just then, someone yelled, "Katie-Skatie!" That was weird, because the only ones who ever called me that were Rachel and Mary. They must have come to the practice to surprise me!

But I looked around and didn't see them. In fact, the voice appeared to have come from a very tall girl with bright red hair, a zillion freckles, and a purple sweatshirt. I didn't want to stare, but then she said it again. "Katie-Skatie!"

She dribbled the ball over to me, singing, "Katie-Skatie is a lady who runs so fast and thinks she's great-y!" She bounced a Figure 8 between her legs, and then bounced the ball to me, which of course I caught, because quick passes are my specialty. She tapped her hands on her chest, a sign for me to pass it back. I did, and then she ran it in a circle around me, laughing. Then she stopped and held the ball.

"Katie-Skatie! It's *me*! Grace!" She bounced the ball to me again, and then I suddenly remembered her.

I bounced the ball back and sang, "Gracey-Lacey with the funny facey. Runs herself all over the placey!"

She started to laugh. "Not just me—me and the ball nowadays!" And again, she did the Figure 8.

Grace Holleman had been in school with Rachel, Mary, and me from pre-school up until third grade, when her family moved. We swore we'd keep in touch, but then things got busy, and we just lost touch.

But she had been one of our best friends, and the four of us used to hang out 24/7. Grace always thought of the best games and was a barrel of fun. And of course I didn't recognize her—when she moved away she had been the littlest girl in the class, a tiny little pipsqueak with bright red hair. (And, honestly kind of a spaz—hence, the song.) How awesome to see not only a familiar face, but to find a long-lost friend.

But before we could catch up, the coach blew a whistle and told us to line up.

They made us do a couple of passing drills and some lay-ups, and eventually we had to count off and play a scrimmage. Grace and I were both evens.

At the end of the practice, they made us run some laps. Grace whispered to me as we ran, "More torture before the final executions." It reminded me how funny she always had been.

When I finally got home, it was almost 8:30, and I was pretty beat. Grace and I had both made the team! Thankfully, it was a Friday and I didn't have homework or school the next day. I was so wrecked, I just wanted to hit the shower and go to bed. But it was still Halloween, so I looked out the window at the kids walking on the street with their candy bags. I looked in the corner by the door for the candy bowl. It was there, but just one measly sourball was in it—and to really rub it in, it was lemon, my least favorite flavor. Oh, well.

At least I had gotten Grace's email address, her phone number, her snail mail, and her mom's cell—I wasn't taking any chances of losing her again! And I was totally psyched to tell the girls about my glorious find.

I didn't have to wait long, because who should come running down from upstairs but three Charlie's Angels: Rachel as Alex, Mary as Natalie, and my blond cocker spaniel, Winnie, dressed as Dylan!

"Hello, Angel!" they sang in deep "Charlie" voices.

It was so sweet, I felt like crying. I had been thinking about this night as my last Halloween—my last chance to get a bunch of free candy—and instead, I got something even better. You can't exactly say that I learned about "the true spirit of Halloween," but I definitely was reminded about the true meaning of best friends.

I told them about seeing Grace again and about how she's called Spacey-Gracey now because she is a) tall enough to actually seem like she's in space, and b) has the crazy idea that she wants to be an astronaut. I also told them about how she had called me Katie-Skatie, which reminded me that we used to call Mary Scary-Mary—a name that seemed quite fitting—it *was* Halloween, after all!

Rachel got quiet all the sudden. Mary asked, "What's the matter, Rach? Aren't you glad that we found Spacey-Gracey-Lacey again? We'll all be able to get together again, just like in the old days."

"Yeah, I know. It's just..."

"What's the problem?" I asked.

She finally burst out, "What the heck rhymes with Rachel?"

Skater Girl

LIESE SHERWOOD-FABRE

Ann Miller wants to make a new start as "Cat," a cool skater, instead of the nerd she was at her old school. She'll be able to learn how to use a skateboard in a couple of weeks...right?

My first-day-of-school outfit was so clean it squeaked. My red Roxy T-shirt was just long enough to meet dress-code standards and matched the shoestrings in my Etnies sneakers. I had spent all summer assembling it, buying one piece at a time as I earned the money babysitting bratty Timmy down the street. But it was worth it. I looked as tight as the pros on the skate videos.

We had moved at the end of last school year, and I had promised myself my eighth-grade year was going to be different. I wanted a new image for my new school. I was going to be a skater, and I attacked this goal the same way I did my school papers— through research. I studied skater videos, magazines, and catalogues to make sure I knew the vocabulary, the moves, and the look.

The only thing I couldn't quite get was the skating part. The minute I got on the board, it went one way and I went another.

But you don't have to skate to look the part, I assured myself on the way to school. *After all, they aren't going to let you skate in school.*

I just made sure the board strapped to my backpack and thunked me on the head with every step, so I looked like I used it. I had worn down the board's edges with sandpaper and my Etnies on the cement. I must have gotten it right because I could feel everyone checking me out at the school's entrance.

Unfortunately, the principal also noticed me. He was standing just inside the building, under a big yellow banner announcing, "Welcome to Thomas G. Harding Middle School." He stopped me as soon as I came through the front door.

"Good morning, Miss...?" he said.

"Miller. Cat Miller."

He raised his eyebrows. My name wasn't really Cat, but I thought it fit my new image better than Ann. There is no way "Ann" would be cool.

"Well...er...Cat. You appear not to be aware of the school policy regarding unauthorized athletic equipment."

Unauthorized athletic equipment? He had to be kidding.

"No Frisbees, skateboards, roller blades..." he was droning on. "Since it's your first day, I won't call your parents this time. Just leave it in the office, okay? You can pick it up after school."

I followed him to the office, pleased to see everybody watching me and the principal. I was getting a rep already.

Things got even better after leaving my board in the office, which, by the way, made my backpack much lighter. When I left the office, a really cool-looking dude in a D.C. Shoes T-shirt gave me a "thumbs-up" before walking away. He sagged his jeans and wore his blond hair long but all flattened out on the sides and flipped out at the bottom, like a knit cap had pushed it down. They probably didn't allow beanies anymore than they did skateboards.

The same guy showed up in my math class. He was sitting in the back of the room, and waved at me to sit by him. I hesitated for a second. I always sat in the front, but I reminded myself that that was the old me—the brainy nerd. Skaters sit in the back.

"I'm Jeremy," he said with a smile that made me curl my toes inside my Etnies.

"Cat," I told him.

"What'd old Wilkens say to you this morning?" he asked.

"Just that I had to leave my board in the office and could pick it up after school."

"Don't let him bug you," he said. "He doesn't like us skaters. He says we mark up the sidewalk and rails around the stairs outside."

Before I could reply, the bell rang. I missed the first few things the teacher announced about the class because all I could hear was Jeremy saying "us skaters."

What I did next almost ruined it all. The teacher put a problem on the board, and without thinking, my hand shot up, and I shouted out the answer. Everybody looked at me with open mouths, and I sank into my seat, wishing I could pull my T-shirt over my head and hide. *Were skaters supposed to do well in math?* I would have to work harder at keeping the old me from appearing.

But maybe it was okay to be a skater *and* good at math. At

lunch, Jeremy called me over to his table and introduced me to his friends. They just accepted me as one of them, even when Jeremy said, "You should have seen her in math class. She smoked the teacher on the first problem."

"You're good in math?" asked Brent, a short, red-haired boy.

I bit my lip to keep from declaring, *Sure. I won the district competition last year.* Instead, I said, "I guess we just covered more in my old school last year."

I was feeling pretty confident until Cecilia, a girl with short, brown-and-black streaked hair asked, "You want to skate with us after school? You have your board with you, right?"

My heart gave a thud. I hadn't considered anyone *inviting* me to skate. I quickly came up with an excuse. "I have to get home after school. My mom's expecting me."

What a muff, I thought. *Only dorks' mothers make them come home after school.*

"Yeah," said Jeremy. "My mom's the same way. You'd think she still thought I was ten."

"You know what my mother did yesterday?" Brent asked with a sad nod, and the conversation took off about mothers and the things they make us do. I was saved. The idea of going someplace to skate after school never came up again.

By the end of school, I was flying. I had a whole new group of friends. Cool friends, not at all like the rejects from my last school. Brent had the same social studies class as I did, and Jeremy showed up in my language arts class. Two classes with Jeremy. What more could I have asked for?

I discovered the answer to that question after picking up my board from the principal's office. They were all there—Jeremy, Brent, Cecilia, and some other skater types, sitting on the steps in front of the school. Jeremy stood up as soon as he saw me.

"Can I see your board?" he asked after he introduced me to the kids I hadn't met before.

I tried to think of something to get me out of this. He would have to know that I had worn it down with sandpaper. My mind froze. I could not even make my mouth say anything more than, "Er," before he took it from me and flipped it over to expose the underside. I had managed to mark it up some, but I knew he could tell it was faked.

"Not bad," he said.

My brain switched on. "Thanks," I said, beginning to catch some momentum. "I've been thinking about getting another. This one's getting kind of old."

"Nah, you can still use it."

He put it on the ground and rolled it a little. Stepping on the end, he flipped it up and grabbed hold of the top part. *How could he make it look so natural?* If I stepped on the end of it, I'd whack some part of my body. You'd be surprised how much that hurts. I walked down the steps, hoping to get away. No such luck.

"What kind of stunts can you do?" asked Brent.

I shrugged. "The usual, ollie, hand-grab, you know, nothing special."

"You go to parks much?" asked a new boy named Sam.

The name of all the skateparks I had so carefully researched in the Yellow Pages fled my memory. "I...uh...I prefer to just skate around town," I managed to stammer out.

"Like where?" he asked, leaning forward on his elbows.

"Well, I haven't had much of a chance here. I've been busy babysitting. In fact, I have to get over there now."

"So, you gonna skate home?" Brent asked. I could detect some skepticism in his voice.

"Nah. I just thought I'd walk. My leg's a little sore. I fell the other day."

"Then why'd you bring the board to school?" This Brent guy was beginning to get on my nerves.

"Well, it, like, didn't hurt this morning. But it's really bad now," I said, taking a few steps and faking a limp.

Brent stood up and blocked my way. "You know what?" he asked with a sneer. "I think you can't skate. I think you're just a poser."

"I'm *not* a fake. I just hurt my leg."

"Let her go, Brent," Jeremy said. "It doesn't matter. What if she can't skate good? No big deal, dude."

"No," he said. "I wanna see her skate."

I glanced back at Jeremy, still standing at the top of the stairs. There was a wide concrete ledge along the steps. It wasn't very long or steep. All I had to do was to stand on the board and ride it down. I could do it. I couldn't let Jeremy know I really was a poser. How could I be so stupid? But it was too late. I either had to go through with it, or plan to come to school tomorrow in last-year's school clothes.

"All right," I said with defiance. "I'll skate. I'll show you."

I dropped my backpack to the ground with a thud, and stamped back up the steps, pushing past Brent. Placing the board on the ground next to the stairs' edge, I put one foot on the board. I swallowed. It looked a lot higher from up here. I moved it back and forth, lining it up to go straight down the edge.

"Come on," Brent challenged. I wanted to skate over his foot.

"Just, like, give me a minute," I said.

Taking a deep breath, I pushed off with my other foot. The flight was exhilarating for a brief moment. Air rushed past my cheeks and pushed the bangs back from my forehead. Then, I felt a growing fear in the pit of my stomach. I knew I was losing control. At the bottom, the board flew up, and I landed hard on my rear. The jolt made my teeth crack together.

But the board continued. It made an arc over the sidewalk, the strip of grass between the sidewalk and the parking lot, and flew end-first into the windshield of a parked car. For a split second, no one said a thing, then the car's alarm screeched to life.

I was still trying to get to my feet when the entire school faculty rushed out the front door. Mr. Wilkens' mouth dropped open and his face turned a bright red.

"My car!" he screamed over the alarm. "My new car!"

He ran to the car, fumbling in his pocket along the way. Pulling out a set of keys, he frantically punched the tiny buttons on the keychain, until the alarm stopped as suddenly as it had begun.

After brushing off my pants, I walked over to my backpack. I could feel the gaze of everyone watching me. The skateboard made the car look like it was sticking its tongue out at Mr. Wilkens. He pulled the board out, and the windshield collapsed into the car.

"Let's go inside," he said, turning to look at me. His voice quivered. "We'll call your parents."

I rubbed my backside tenderly, and limped up the stairs behind Mr. Wilkens. Somehow, I knew I wasn't getting my board back this time. Not that I would be able to use it anyway. I was sure my parents would ground me until college.

An hour later, I let myself into the house. I knew what my parents told me over the phone in Mr. Wilkens' office was only the beginning of the lecture I would hear when they got home. I would be seeing a lot of that brat Timmy to earn the money to pay for Mr. Wilkens' windshield. Not that it mattered. I wouldn't be able to do anything else, being grounded for the next month. The worst part was I had ruined my cool image before I had a chance to enjoy it.

The doorbell rang just as I was about to sit down and drown my sorrows in a mega-sized bowl of rocky road ice cream. I pulled myself carefully off the couch. I was pretty sure I had seriously damaged my tailbone. I almost dropped my ice cream when I saw Jeremy on my doorstep.

"Hi," I said. *Was that all I could come up with?*

"Hi. I just wanted to know if you were okay."

"I'm fine. My butt hurts some, but I'll be okay. My pride's hurt more than anything."

"I just wanted to tell you...." He glanced down at his shoes.

"Yeah?"

"Just that...it took courage to try and skate when you don't know how."

"Thanks."

"I thought...maybe...I could show you how to skate."

"That'd be nice. Of course, it'll be a while. I'm gonna be grounded for the next month."

"Well, when your parents allow it, I thought I could show you some basics."

"Thanks. I'd let you in, but my parents will be here soon, and—"

"It's okay. I just...." He scuffed his toe on the door mat. "Could you help me with math?"

"Huh?"

"Do you think your parents would let you help me with my math homework?"

"I don't know," I said slowly. Inside, my heart was pounding so fast, I was sure he could see the Roxy logo on my shirt jump.

"Oh," he said, turning to go.

"But I can ask them," I said quickly. "I mean, they might think it was good for me to help someone. I'll let you know."

"Cool. Well, see ya."

I closed the door and leaned against it. Maybe being a brain wasn't that bad.

Best Friends and Dog Biscuits

KRISTEN KEMP

Kandi's got to figure out which is more important...
making the cheerleading team, or keeping a friend
she's known practically her whole life.

I might actually make it for cheerleading this year—only because Mishra, the Class Acrobat, dislocated her something-or-other and Aimee, the teen model at FlorMart, transferred to a private school. That means there are two open spots on the eighth-grade squad. The other four will definitely go to Erica, Lilly, Brooke, and my kinda-sorta-yes-maybe best friend Suze, pronounced Sooz, like Underoos. I swear, one of those spots will be mine, mine, mine.

And when I get determined, oh, buddy, watch out. Once, I even told Andrew Green that I would eat my Chihuahua's Beggin' Strips, and he didn't believe me. I proved him wrong (then barfed, but that's not the point), and we've been talking more ever since. That is good because he's cute—seriously, I wish I could stop dreaming about him. Another example: When I told Suze I was giving our science teacher a can of squirt cheese for Christmas last year, she didn't think I'd do it. I really did, and Mr. Cohen wound up giving me a B instead of the C+ that I deserved. Score. Suze says I'm developing problems. I say that Suze has the sense of humor of a soap dish—especially lately.

But regardless of our differences, we both love cheerleading. She's *so* good at it. For me, I love it mostly because I like being the center of attention. Everyone eyes the squad when they wear their uniforms to school on game days. But I haven't told Suze this. It would make her less enthusiastic about sharing her cheerleading secrets. She knows I have the willpower to make the squad; I just need the skills. That's a problem because I am about as limber as a concrete sidewalk—and for tryouts, I will have to do the splits. So for the next seven days, with Suze's perky coaching abilities, I will force my you-know-what closer and closer to the floor, defying gravity and testing the limits of human anatomy.

Oh, and the actual cheers are troublesome, too. On Tuesday, Suze made flashcards to help me memorize them. You'd think I'd have them down by now, considering that I've attended every Prattville Middle School basketball game since the sixth grade. Suze always wanted me to attend, so I did. Now, she's really coming through for me, even though I know she's a little concerned. She wants us to cheer together. She just doesn't want to see me upset if

I don't make it again—which, darn it, I will, or I swear I'll eat more dog treats.

It's Thursday morning, between first and second periods, and Suze asked me, "Kandi, do you want to spend the night Saturday?" Then she started whistling the theme to Sesame Street, her gray eyes wide and her head cocked to the left.

I felt guilty when I answered, "Yeah, maybe. Let me think about it." Then I high-tailed it away from my locker, acting like I was in a hurry to get to class, even though the whole world—*especially* Suze—knows I'm always late.

I hate myself for getting so irritated with her lately, but I get irritated anyway. First of all, she just tattooed a childish theme song onto my brain. Second, she spoke in her high, goofy voice, the one she uses when she talks to her guinea pig named Ernie. Suze even uses the voice in public, like when she called her mom on the cafeteria pay phone yesterday during lunch. That's the third thing that's been wearing me out: Mrs. Quick—Suze's mom—never lets her go anywhere, except to school or events *at* the school. As a direct result, she hasn't been to a slumber party in over a year because she's never allowed to go. Can I just tell you that I'm sick to death of watching G-rated movies while we dress Ernie up in Strawberry Shortcake outfits? Does this make me a bad person?

Now that the seventh grade is almost over, I need to move on up. I'm finally wearing contact lenses, and I recently started buying form-fitting clothes instead of baggier ones. When I brought my new clothes over to Suze's house to show her recently, she turned cranberry-juice red. After seeing my new purple tank top, she exclaimed, "It's so low cut! Are you sure that's ethical?" At that moment, her favorite sweatshirt, the one with the teddy bears on it, really bugged me. Again, I felt guilty when I thought, *She needs to grow up.*

Sara, a girl from the volleyball team, never acts childish and she always wears tank tops. She and I have been hanging out more lately. We met because her last name is Christopher and mine is Christian, so we wound up sitting next to each in typing and in gym. A few Fridays ago, we even went to the mall together. We hung out at the food court with Andrew and his skater friends. Suze had been feeling left out because of Sara, so to spare her feelings, I told her I was spending the evening at the nursing home with my grandmother.

Of course, the following Monday at school, Suze busted me during English. Her note said:

How could you?

The nerves in my skin went tingly—exactly like the time when I was ten and my mom asked me if I'd been lopping mud pies at parked cars on Eighth Street. I swore to her that I would never do such a thing. A few minutes later, Mom handed me the phone, and my aunt advised me to tell the truth because she'd spent five minutes scraping a mud glob off her brand new Buick. My aunt had seen me cackling with my neighbor at the scene of the crime.

Just like in the pie incident, Suze had caught me with, um, dirt on my hands. I wrote back:

I didn't. I mean, I Wait, what exactly did I do?

Her return note said:

You know what you did. Or maybe I should say what you didn't do—you didn't go see your grandmother.

I nervously responded:

Crap. You're right. I didn't. I'm sorry.

In florescent pink pen, she wrote back:

I'm sorry, too. I'm sorry that Sara is cooler than me and that you want to chase Andrew, and that Ernie and I aren't good enough for you anymore. I wish I could be someone better than me, but I can't. Still BFF? SuzeQ

I replied:

Ugh. It was low. I am low. I am lower than lower than low. It was a hateful thing to do, and I wouldn't be surprised if you hated me. I owe you a big sincere sorry. And I'm sorry, sorry, sorry. Yes, BFF!

At the time, I was lucky she was willing to forgive me; that she still thought of me as friend-worthy. I had been a dawg, and I wasn't proud of it. But I don't want to dwell on that moment.

Later that day at lunch, I noticed Suze was wearing her half of our best friends necklace—I had totally forgotten about it. Just as I was about to ask her about it, Andrew came over to ask me a question, and I found that I was embarrassed by her. She was sitting to my right, wearing a sweater with apples on it, and talking to this guy Marc who carries a briefcase and speaks as if he doesn't have nasal passages. (Suze and Marc have a friendly competition for first chair in their band class.) At that moment, when I was trying to impress my crush, I longed for Sara instead of Suze. How bad am I to not be ashamed, even though Suze has helped me with my splits all week long? I am nothing but a canine. Woof.

Suze and I'd had a good run, though. We met at sixth grade cheerleading tryouts, back when I still believed she was the coolest, funniest girl ever. She was a double-jointed gymnast who clapped her hands with bubbly enthusiasm even when she wasn't cheering. She practically had a photographic memory and never messed up any lines or movements in the routines.

When I started the sixth grade, I thought becoming a cheerleader could improve my social status (and my social skills). After all, I had a natural love for yelling and screaming. So I tried out for the squad just like I had every year since the first grade in the hopes that things would get better. The girls named Erica, Lilly, Brooke, Mishra, Aimee, and Suze were sure things; they had the highest side hurdles anyone had ever seen. But Suze didn't fit in with them, and we naturally found each other. Together, we tried again in the seventh grade. She tried to teach me some cheer about a barnyard, but I kept yelling *cow* when I was supposed to be saying *wow*. When I didn't make it, she bought two boxes of tissues and gave me a mechanical Tasmanian Devil sucker.

She has practiced with me ever since, and I have improved—well, a little. I just feel like this year is cheerleading destiny. And maybe, if Suze and I are on the squad together, our friendship will get better, instead of falling apart like it is right now.

"Kandi, what about Saturday?" Suze asked me again. It was Friday after last period. She was carrying around a book called *Get Your Guinea Pig to Perform Tricks* in plain view.

"I have to visit my grandmother. Really, this time, I do," I said, crossing my fingers behind my back, hoping to be forgiven for lying again. Andrew and his friends asked Sara and me to the movies Saturday night. And let me tell you, I want to hang out with them almost as much as I want to make the squad. Maybe even more.

Suze put her pointer finger on her temple and made a wrinkled-up, cross-eyed face. "Dagnabbers!" she squealed. "You'd better not be lying this time. You wouldn't do that, would you?"

"*Never*," I answered, feeling like the mud pie that I was.

"You're still coming over Sunday though, right? Tryouts are Monday—if you're really sure you want to go through it again. You have been doing the splits every day, haven't you?"

"Every day," I was *not* lying this time. "But the only kind of splits I like are the banana kind."

She laughed, and I forced a smile.

"Just be there by noon, Kandi," she said in baby talk. "That doesn't mean 1 P.M."

"Okay," I said. "Yes, okay."

"Tell your Granny I said hi, and ringy dingy me tomorrow," she added, bouncing away down the hall toward the exit.

✿ ✿ ✿

Somehow, I managed to have a pretty good time on Saturday even though I had ditched my kinda-sorta-yes-maybe best friend. Andrew put his arm around me during the movie, which I totally didn't pay attention to because a) uh, his arm was around me, b) I couldn't stop talking, and c) the stupid insides of my legs were so sore from doing the splits that it hurt when I sat still. Sara got along great (really great!) with Andrew's best friend Jeremy, and a bunch of us ate pizza together afterward. When I was standing outside waiting for my mom to pick us up, Andrew pulled me to the side and told me he wanted to go out again. My insides churned in delicious ways, and I said, "Yeah, okay." I asked Sara to spend the night so we could discuss things I could never share with Suze. I finally fell asleep with a sense of something authentic, and I had never experienced that before.

Late Sunday morning, I woke up with far less self-assurance. I was overwhelmed with shame at my behavior toward Suze. Once I got to Suze's house, I told her that my grandmother said hi—that wasn't lying, I *did* go see Nana on Saturday morning. Suze believed me, and thankfully, she was too busy cleaning Ernie's cage to ask about the rest of my weekend. I calmed down. She made me stretch out, so my inner thighs felt better. After jumps and chants, we did splits. I forced myself to go lower, believing that I deserved pain for lying to Suze. Then we went over the Cat Shake cheer, and I didn't mess up the words even once. That's because I'd been studying Suze's flashcards.

When I arrived at tryouts Monday after school, Suze handed me a teddy bear bordered envelope. Inside, it said, "*GOOO* Kandi!" She hugged me, and we went in, promising to do our best. It was clear from the start that I was in trouble. There were many girls, but two unexpected ones, Jenny and Adonna, who had skills that definitely rivaled mine. I watched them nail everything, and I wanted to cry because I wasn't going to make it. Again. I was the third best with only two spots left.

When it was over, Suze squeezed me and said sweet things in the same tone she uses on Ernie. She is kind, I know, but her voice is like a cheese-grater slicing through my patience.

Tuesday, Suze didn't show up at school. I tried calling her during lunch. I wanted to tell her that she'd better get her booty into school so she didn't miss the last day of tryouts. I assumed she was sick, and I planned to give her such a good pep talk so she'd magically feel well again. I wanted to do anything I could for her because I'd been such a lousy friend. But there was no answer at her house—she couldn't be on the squad if she missed tryouts!

I kept thinking she'd show up in the gym after school, even though technically, if she didn't attend classes that day, she wouldn't be allowed to try out. The cheerleading coach adored Suze—just like all of our other teachers do—and they'd probably make an exception for her. I watched Erica, Lilly, and Brooke perform. It's no surprise that those girls managed to stay confident; they're always perfect, never goofing up even once. Jenny and Adonna and some others didn't do as well as they had done the day before. It looked to me like their willpower was fading. I pumped myself up with thoughts of dog biscuits and squirt cheese, and my own determination returned.

I was the last one to go. I was only a half-inch off the floor during my splits, it felt like I made it ten feet up in the air during my side hurdle, and I nailed the Cat Shake cheer. When I finished, I expected Suze to be there cheering me on. She's the only one who'd understand how on top of the world I felt. Whether I got on the squad or not, I had done a good job. Suze was the person I wanted to share that awesome feeling with.

When I got home, I left a message on her answering machine. I was concerned—what if she had chicken pox? What if Ernie had jumped out her bedroom window or something? And what was she going to do about missing tryouts? That last one was the most important question, the one I simply couldn't get out of my head. But she wasn't there. I began to worry about Suze. I didn't sleep well—and it wasn't because of the pain in my inner thighs.

Wednesday morning, the coach posted the new eighth grade squad on the door of the principal's office. I was on the list, and Suze was not. The best thing ever—the one thing I'd always wanted in addition to you-know-who (Andrew)—had happened. But I wasn't happy. I felt kind of sick inside. Something was missing. While I stared at the list, my eyes got watery, and I didn't understand why.

"I did it for you."

I turned around to see Suze. Her smile was bigger than ever, but something behind her gray eyes looked sad. She said, "Don't look so surprised," handing me what I knew would be a congrats card. If it had teddy bears on it, I didn't notice.

"Why on earth would you do something like—"

"—if I had tried out, you wouldn't have made it," Suze said. She wasn't wearing her pink bow, and she wasn't talking in the guinea pig voice.

"You did this for me?" I asked slowly.

"Yes, I did. You think this will make you happy, and well, I want you to be happy. So, well, oops!" she exclaimed, switching to Ernie speak. "I just had the worst cold yesterday! Dagnabbers!"

She skipped school and tryouts just for me? She knew and I knew that I didn't deserve such a favor. I looked down at my tennis shoes, new red and white ones that would look good with my cheer uniform.

"What did you tell your mom?" I asked. She never pulled fast ones on Mrs. Quick.

"I told her that I was sick, and that I didn't care if I was on the squad or not."

"But you're really good at cheerleading!"

"Nah, it's not really my thing anymore," she explained, and I thought about how she was more into getting As and playing her clarinet lately. She liked the athletic part of cheerleading, not the social part. But still, this was surprising news. "If we weren't going to be on it together, I just don't give a crap," she added.

"So you—"

"Yes," she said, looking around the hallway to make sure no one was listening to our conversation. "I fibbed."

Finally, I managed to say, "You little liar, you."

"Hey, I learned from the master," she said in an icicle voice.

When it became obvious that she knew I lied to her again last weekend, my skin went tingly. I had really dug myself in good this time. Meanwhile, there was a long pause between us. I waited for her to rail into me—she had every right. But she didn't. She was just quiet. In the silence, it occured to me: I didn't have to keep being such an awful friend. I could take some cues from her and try to make things right. So instead of wallowing in guilt, I had another idea. I touched her shoulder and said, "Listen, Suze..."

"Yeah?"

"Do you want to go to the movies this weekend with Sara and Jeremy and Andrew and me? Marc can come, too," I offered. Maybe she'd like to be included in my evolving life. I realized I'd been underestimating her. She was just trying to grow up, too.

"Really?" she asked, sounding perkier, more like herself.

"Yeah, it would be fun," I said, hugging her.

"Maybe," she answered. "Yeah."

I started thinking that friends like Suze were rare, and I'd better do what I could to hang on to her. Then I noticed she was not wearing her BFF necklace, and I felt bad and sad. I became determined to be good—to make her want to wear it again. "Come on. Come with us," I said, already brainstorming ways we could convince her mom to let her go. "You'll come?"

"If I can, yes," she said as she checked her watch. I knew she didn't want to be late to class. She waved goodbye and disappeared into the mobs of kids in the hallway.

Now, I had a new mission. I would make sure Suze was also happy.

Pretty Much Completely

KATE HILL CANTRILL

How do you know if you're a popular girl or one of the weirdos?
In the lunchroom, you've got to choose where you sit!

I was the new girl in school and completely terrified. It's hard starting over in a new place, and all I did that first day was miss my old school and my old friends. As I walked into my new homeroom for the first time, I held back tears, wishing I could turn back time to when my parents were still married and I was back home with my real friends.

As I sat down at an empty desk, a strange girl tapped me on the back and said, "Hey." I turned around and smiled, and she must have seen that I was terrified because she said, "Don't worry, there's only one first day of school every year." She was sucking on a lollipop and was dressed half punk-rock and half just-weird, with ripped man-pants and little plastic rats glued to her denim jacket. She wasn't what you'd call a *natural* beauty, but I thought she'd look better if she toned it down a bit, maybe put on a simple pair of faded jeans. Maybe wear a bracelet or two.

"Thanks," I replied. "My name's Vanessa."

"I'm Dawn."

Just then, two girls in the back started arguing and calling each other names, and everyone turned to look. Dawn must have seen how shocked I was by some of the names they called each other because she said, "Girls didn't fight in your old school?" I shook my head. In my mind, I cursed my mother for divorcing my father. If they had stayed together, I would have been at my old school. I wouldn't care how much they argued. I'd just stay in my room and play retro CDs.

The bell rang and I checked my schedule for my first class.

"At lunch," Dawn said, "meet me by the statue down the hall. You can sit with me."

"Thanks," I said, and I meant it because, man oh jeez, I was not looking forward to the lunch thing, as everyone knows the lunch thing is the worst thing of all.

That morning, I noticed that there were a few girls in the school that seemed like me, looked like me, but what was I supposed to do? I couldn't very well walk up to one and say, "Hey, I noticed that you, too, understand the importance of simple yet playful accessorizing." That would be ridiculous! I knew that those sorts of things take time, and at least I had someone to sit with at lunch that day. At least I wouldn't have to choke down a pizza slice while hiding in the bathroom. I wouldn't be alone.

At lunch, Dawn sat us at a table in the corner.

"We sat here all last year," she said, and I was glad to hear her say 'we' to know that others would be coming. When the others came, though, I wasn't so sure anymore. Her friends were just as random as Dawn's clothes. One girl who called herself Raz wore thick glasses that pressed into the bridge of her nose and a button that said, "Bugs Make the World Go Round." Another girl brought a cello to the table and actually sat it in its own seat. There were two boys, too, who seemed normal except that they communicated in a made-up language that they called *Zok*. It sounded sort of like English but with extra zs. *Letzok eatzok*, for instance, meant *chow down*.

It seemed pretty evident to me that this was the catch-all table; the place where all the misfits sat.

Wow, I thought. *I've never been a misfit before.* I looked around the cafeteria, and I longed to be sitting at a different table, with people I would have more in common with. I looked down at my clogs, tapped them together, and wished to be back at my old school. But of course, I was still there, and just quietly ate my lunch.

The next week at school, I had a brilliant idea descend upon my brain. It happened when I was watching a group of girls—a group that was obviously the well-adjusted popular group—sitting around in the school yard. I noticed that they seemed popular because they matched—not their shoes to their bags, but to each other. It seemed like such a simple thing, so I located Dawn and said that I wanted to hang out with her after school.

"What are we going to do?" she asked.

"Shop," I said.

"I only shop in thrift stores," she said.

"Not anymore."

Dawn seemed to be uncomfortable at the stores we went into. She'd just stand there with her thumbs hooked inside the waistband of the man-pants she was wearing. I had to basically, pretty much, do everything. I got her dressed in some normal clothes, finally, and pushed her in front of the mirror. She looked pretty good. She looked even better when I wiped the dark lipstick off of her and replaced it with Cherry-Hint Pucker Gloss.

"There," I said. "What do you think?"

"I don't know what I think," she said.

"Why not?"

"Because I'm no longer here. I don't know where I've gone," she pointed at the mirror. "Because that's not me." She removed the clothes and put her oversized pants back on, and we looked instantly out of whack again, like two pieces from a different puzzle trying to jam into the same slot.

On the way home, I couldn't help it—I started to cry. I couldn't tell Dawn I was crying over her man-pants and split-ends, so I just shrugged when she asked me what was wrong.

"I understand," she said.

"You do?" I wiped my eyes on my sleeve.

"It's really traumatic to start at a new school," she said. "It's like you're a fish tossed into a brand new sea, and everything—the waves, the whales, the reefs—are totally different from what you've known. It sure is lucky you found me because I'm the fish *in the know*. Soon, everything will feel familiar again."

I thought I had just been crying about man-pants and lip gloss; but once she said I felt like a fish in a brand-new sea, I started to cry about that. I thought about my old school. I thought about how I could have walked through those halls with my eyes squeezed shut and I wouldn't have bumped into anything. I thought of how I used to walk down the hall between classes and people I knew would call out my name and say *Hello*, or slap me a high 5, or tug sweetly on my hair, or just meet my eyes and smile. I thought of all of that and I cried.

Dawn put her arm around me and said, "Let it out. Don't hold back or care what people think. Just remember that everyone has been sad about something at some point, so they'll understand."

I didn't hold back. In fact, I cried until I got home, and then I cried until the sun went down.

My mother didn't bother me at all when I got home. The only thing she did was slip a note under my door that said, "I (heart) you so much it makes my eyeballs ache," and that actually made me laugh a little. She can be cute when she tries to cheer me up.

The next day at lunch, the girl named Raz with the heavy glasses brought a little goldfish bowl to the table. Inside of it was one of her pet bugs.

"Letzok seezok," one of the Zok boys said. "Coolzok."

When Raz asked if I wanted to take a closer look at "Bugzander" (this was what she called it, no lie), I just shook my head and crossed my fingers under the table that no one else in the lunchroom would notice her weird pet on our table. Fat chance.

I almost slid off my seat when one of the girls from the normal (some said popular) table came over and asked what it was. She shook her pint of chocolate milk and stared into the glass. Her name was Bridget. I recognized her from the second row in my Algebra class.

"You really have a bug in there?" she asked Raz, who nodded. "What if it gets out?"

"It won't get out," Raz said.

"But what if it does?"

"I'll catch it, no problem."

Bridget laughed and looked at everyone at the table. "If I sat here, I'd make sure my sandwich didn't have any special visitors on it before I chomped it."

"Hah hah," Raz said sarcastically.

"Don't worry about us, Bridget," Dawn said. "We could use the protein."

"Not funny!" Raz said, as she pulled Bugzander closer to her.

Before Bridget headed back to that glorious table that didn't have bugs on it, she stopped and looked at me. "You're in my Algebra class aren't you?"

I nodded.

"Cool clogs."

I looked at her feet. We were wearing the same exact shoes.

Dawn must have noticed that I watched Bridget walk back to her table because she said, "Dullsville, man. Total snore-fest. That's all they talk about: Shoes. Shoes and boys who wear baseball caps. It makes me bored just thinking about it." She yawned and I did too, but only because you can't watch someone yawn without doing so yourself. I thought talking about shoes and boys who wear baseball caps sounded pretty okay. I checked my sandwich for movement and, finding no strange visitors, I ate it.

I remember a new girl that came to my old school the year before. She was small and kind-looking and very shy—this I knew because of how she held her shoulders slumped, and not because I had ever talked to her. I would have talked to her. I should have said hello and asked her how she was doing. I should have told her a funny story, or, better yet, I should have asked her to tell me one about her old school. I should have laughed hard and said, "That's a very funny story. Boy, you must really miss that place," and when she would have nodded, or shrugged, or cried a little, I would have touched her arm and invited her to eat lunch with me. It was just something I hadn't thought about before—how important those little things mean when you're the brand spanking new kid.

Perhaps Bridget *did* think about that stuff because the next day in Algebra, Bridget said, "Hey," when she walked by my desk. I was caught off guard and sort of snorted. After class, though, I walked over to her and said, "Boy, this class is pretty hard."

She agreed by rolling her eyes and then she said, "Listen, we should study together and stuff."

"Definitely," I said.

"Absolutely," she said. "Listen, come sit with us at lunch today and we'll work it out. Okay?"

I nodded and nearly freaked out almost completely. I had an invitation to sit at the normal (some said *popular*) table!

Later, in the cafeteria, after I placed my backpack at my new table, I found Dawn and told her that I was going to sit with Bridget because of Algebra. "It's like our teacher has it in for us, Dawn. It's so hard! I'm so lucky to know someone in my class, you know?"

Dawn just said, "Yep," and walked away toward the misfits. I felt bad, but what was I supposed to do?

"You shouldn't have lied," my mother said that night when I told her that I thought Dawn was acting a little unreasonable.

"But mom, this is my *future* we're talking about! My math grade!"

"Oh, really? How much time did you spend talking about math at your new table?" she asked.

"A lot," I said, which was only half true. Actually, it wasn't true at all because math never came up. Instead, we talked about, well, a boy who wore a baseball cap who Bridget liked. Still, I felt like it helped me to focus on my studies—more so than bugs and weird zok noises. I told my mother this, and she just shook her head.

"Dawn was kind to you," she said, "and she deserved the truth."

I didn't sleep well that night because I knew my mom was right. In the morning, I looked for Dawn out on the front steps. I finally saw her crossing the lawn alone. Her feet stomped the grass funny because she was wearing the sort of boots a fly fisher or a plumber in a flooded basement might wear. Weird, but somehow she got away with it. It was obvious that she was planning to walk right by me, but I jumped up and stepped on one of her untied laces and she jerked to a stop.

I told her I was sorry that I left her lunch table. "It's just that I feel comfortable at the other table, Dawn. I really like you, but I just don't fit in with the others."

"That's the point," she said. "None of us fits in. We're okay with it though, because when you hang out with other people who don't fit in, you kind of, well, fit in." With her free foot, she nudged my foot off her lace. "But it's all right with me if you want to sit somewhere else. I just didn't like that you lied to me—I'm not an idiot, you know."

"I know you're not an idiot," I said. "I'm sorry."

"Accepted," she said. She started to walk away, and then she turned and said, "Maybe I can take you to my favorite thrift store sometime? Just for fun?"

"Definitely," I said. "That sounds like a blast." I meant it, too. It sounded like a pretty weird and wonderful thing to do.

At lunch, Bridget and her friends talked about the boy with the baseball cap that Bridget liked. I didn't mind talking about it again—it wasn't super exciting, nor was it going to help me in Algebra class—but it seemed important to Bridget, and she was nice enough to me. Besides, if I ever got bored with the conversation, I could look over at my old table to see what they were up to. Today, it seemed like Raz was showing off her new bee-keeper outfit she had been talking about for weeks. She kept the hat on for the duration of the lunch period; she lifted the netting whenever she needed to take a bite of her sandwich.

"Is that girl going to the moon or something?" Bridget asked when she saw that I was looking at Raz. "She totally looks silly with that space suit on."

Some of the girls at the table laughed.

"It's a bee suit," I said. "Her uncle keeps bees and she's learning how to collect honey from their comb."

"That other girl looks like she's going moon walking, too," said Sally, who sat across from Bridget. "Look at her boots!"

She was talking about Dawn's plumber boots, and I felt a little sick to my stomach when I realized that. I felt compelled to stick up for her. "Dawn feels more comfortable in boy's clothing," I said. "She can sort of pull it off, don't you think?"

They looked at me funny. Funny as in: *Does she fit in here?*

Bridget was looking at me funny too, but then she smiled and said, "Yeah, she *does* pull it off. I know I couldn't, but she does, so that's cool."

"I guess," Sally said. "It does look kind of cool, I guess. It just surprised me."

"She *is* surprising," I said. I half-smiled at Bridget to let her know that I appreciated her saying what she did. I knew that sometimes she could be a little dull, a little plain vanilla, and maybe even a bit self-absorbed, but basically, I felt pretty comfortable there with her and her friends. And when Dawn caught my eye and blew a sweet air-kiss across the lunchroom, I didn't care who saw, and I felt totally comfortable catching that kiss and blowing one back. It was just how things were, and I figured that was pretty okay.

Fifty Bucks

S.K. Dunn

*Molly's picked up a chunk of change along
with her dog-sitting duties. But can she hold
onto it long enough to make a connection?*

Great ideas seem to come from the strangest places. And even though I have always counted on my BFF Lily to inspire some of my most marvelous and crazy plans, I never expected her dog, Minnie, to change my life.

Okay, so here's the scoop: There are some things in life that you'd only do for your BFF—babysit her monster little cousin, politely eat her mother's vegetarian meatloaf, and walk her dog. Lily had asked me to dog-sit her little pug, Minnie, while she (Lily, not Minnie) went to her swimming quarterfinals.

So there I was at 7:30 in the morning, at the little park on our street, trying to do my doggy-sitting duty (which was waiting for Min-Min to do her, uh...doody). Lily had reminded me at least a zillion times before she left that I had to pick "it" up after Min-Min goes, which I definitely was not looking forward to.

Finally, under a bush near the end of the path, she dropped one. I heaved a sigh, got on my knees, held my breath, and groped Min-Min's business with my plastic-covered hand. And then, right there on the ground, I saw it.

A $50 bill.

That night, my grandmother came over for dinner. She is more of a diamonds-and-pearls type grandmother than the milk-and-cookies variety. When she comes for dinner, we always eat in the fancy dining room, with the fancy china and fancy napkins. The dinner, too, is usually fancy. All of this is because my grandmother is, well, fancy. The dinner conversation is usually pretty formal when she's around and I have a hard time thinking of things to say.

But that night, because I couldn't think of anything else to say, I brought up the news of my good fortune. "I found a fifty-dollar bill today," I said, trying to sound unimpressed.

"Molly, that's a lot of money for someone to lose," my mom said uneasily. "Not enough to report, but enough to make someone's day unpleasant."

"It's not *that* much," I said, probably only half-convincingly. I turned to my grandmother, figuring she would be sympathetic to my point-of-view. "After all, you can't even buy a decent pair of shoes for fifty bucks!" I thought she'd understand this, especially since she wears only designer clothes and gets her nails done every week at a fancy nail salon.

But instead of backing me up, my grandmother, Mrs. Civilized-People-Do-Not-Eat-at-The-Olive-Garden, placed both her palms flat on the table. "Young lady," she huffed, looking at me sternly, "it continues to fascinate me that you seem to know ridiculous ways to spend money, but only have a limited understanding of how one might go about earning it."

I swallowed. I knew she was referring to how I'd quickly spent the money she gave me for my last birthday. Lily and I blew it at the mall—I managed to stretch it through the food court; a couple long, bendy pencils; and a portrait of us dressed in old-timey clothes. I have no clue where that photo is now.

"Think about how you'd feel if you lost fifty dollars," my dad piped in, with that serious, stone-faced look he always does. "Just figure how long it would take you to save up that much."

I gave that some serious thought. I tried to figure out how long it would take me to save $50 from my $10-a-week allowance—minus, of course, the smoothies, new lip gloss, CDs….Really, it was more math than I could calculate without a pen and paper handy.

About a month before our neighborhood pool opens for the summer, the clubhouse opens. Lily and I started to hang out there a few summers ago, and have hung out there ever since. They sell smoothies and flavored coffee drinks, brownies, and snacks that we always buy after school.

It was a warm May day, so we got one of the little tables outside. We each had a Giant Passion fruit smoothie. It was *my* treat, because, even though the two drinks cost my whole allowance, I didn't care—I had $50. When Austin Powell, our class's major cutie, skated up, Lily and I were the only two on the patio.

We all went to school together, but he either didn't recognize us or had decided we weren't cool enough for him to acknowledge our presence. So I decided not to acknowledge his.

Austin pulled out his cell to make a call. I turned to Lily. "How cool is that about the fifty bucks?"

"Very cool," she said, pushing her sunglasses onto her forehead to look at me. "You should save it. Save it up."

Lily has savings savvy. She actually socked away enough to buy herself an iPod. She planned the purchase out carefully, budgeting and disciplining every cent. I, on the other hand, am more of an impulse buyer. Whenever I've wanted something way expensive, I usually just asked my parents for it for a holiday or birthday. "I wouldn't even know what to save for," I said to Lily.

"Oh, c'mon, Molly. Let's think of something—even something crazy."

We were slurping our smoothies and giving this some thought, when the silence was interrupted by an electronic version of *Für Elise*, a song scarred into my brain from years of piano lessons.

We looked toward the gate, where the sound was coming from. It was Austin's cell. I wondered who he was talking to, as he leaned against the gate. It was weird but I was almost (okay, totally) jealous. *He'd never be able to dial me up*, I thought, *even if he wanted to*. That's because my folks refused to get me a cell.

Wait—that was it!

"Lily," I almost yelled. "A cell!"

Now, my parents are kind of strange about the cell phone issue. They think they're way too expensive and la-di-da for a kid to have. My mom has one for business, but that's it. Back when I first asked for one, my dad got me one of those prepaid phones for me to have just for emergencies, but I used up the minutes in like a day talking to Lily. My dad got *sooo* mad when we broke down in his car and he asked to borrow it for a call...and discovered it had no minutes left. My stint as a cell-phone user was over after that.

But I was pretty sure they'd drop the cell-phone restriction as long as it was on my dime. Let the savings begin!

Lily and I went to her house and planned the whole thing. She found a good deal on the Internet where I could get a phone, activation, and the whole set-up for $120—plus, best of all, I could even get a second phone for free for her (who else was I going to talk to?).

That night, my mom came into my room. I was sprawled out on my bed, finishing homework. I non-strategically blurted out, "Can I get a cell phone?"

"We've talked about this," Mom said, patting my shoulder. "They're expensive."

"But Lily and I found a deal on the Internet for one-hundred and twenty-dollars for two phones—everything included! I'll pay for it!"

"Activation?" Mom asked.

"Everything," I said, chewing the inside of my mouth. She let out a breath like she was almost about to give in.

Then she sucked in one bigger than the one she let out and said, "Martha"—never a good sign when she uses my real name—"the expensive part is the monthly fee. You only get a set amount of minutes. After that, you pay a lot."

"How much? Like, a thousand dollars?" I asked with just the right dose of sarcasm.

"With your phone habit, I wouldn't be surprised," she said. "Dad still isn't over your using up that prepaid."

"Yeah, but—"

"Molly," she interrupted, and then smiled to make it nicer. "Good night."

But when I called Lily the next morning to tell her what my mom had said, we came up with Plan B. "Tell her you'll pay for three months in advance, and then if you handle it well—no, say, 'responsibly'—you can keep it."

"Okay," I said. Sometimes, I swear Lily should be a lawyer.

"And, obviously, you have to figure out how much money you need to get started!" Lily added before hanging up.

I hate math, and I knew by the time I calculated it all, I would be in retirement and there would be no point.

Luckily for me, Lily knows me better than anyone. The phone rang. "Molly, you need to save two-hundred and twenty-dollars. Now go talk to them!"

My parents were at the kitchen table when I crashed in. "What if I save up for the phone, and pay for three months in advance? That's two-hundred and twenty-dollars." I paused to catch myself, and added my best and most sincere, "Please?"

I looked at my mom anxiously. My father just looked confused. "Oh, all right!" she finally broke out. "If you get the money, you can get a phone."

That was all I needed to hear.

For the next six weeks, I worked like crazy. School let out for the year, and instead of letting it blow by, the hot summer days seemed to stretch into eternity. On Tuesdays, I babysat for some friends of my parents. On some mornings and afternoons, I walked the weird neighbor's even weirder dog. I even sunk to my absolute lowest, doing Mike Reilly's paper route while he was on vacation.

But forget the work—let's talk about the sacrifice! Instead of spending the $5 my mom gave me every day for the pool's snack bar, I used it at the grocery store and bought things like Fruit Roll-Ups and granola bars to brown-bag. It was cheaper that way and I got to save money.

At first, everybody thought I was kind of a goof for not getting fries and stuff, but then some of them decided to be my "support group." Pretty soon, there was a bunch of us who hung out at the picnic tables instead of the snack bar. The guards called us the Snack Pack, which was pretty funny. Austin even came and sat at the Snack Pack table once, but I could barely talk to him. I prayed it would be easier over the phone—when I got one.

❀ ❀ ❀

One morning, I woke up early to count the money I'd made so far.

Babysitting: $8 X 6 times = $48

Dogwalking: $3 X 24 times = $72

Allowance: $10 X 6 weeks = $60 minus money for snacks= $30

Mike Reilly's paper route = $20

I went straight to the money journal I'd been keeping and added up everything. I stared at the figure. $170!

Not bad but it seemed like I should have more. I'd been working so hard! I figured I still needed $50. I should have been much closer. I stared down at the page, not fully believing. Did anyone still owe me? Was there a job I hadn't added in?

I swallowed the lump in my throat and walked into the kitchen. My mom looked up from her cereal and asked, "What's wrong, Molly? Are you sick?"

I shook my head, fighting the tears that were trying to spring to my eyes. "I only have one-hundred and seventy-dollars. I still need a stupid fifty bucks!" I poured some cereal and milk really fast in hopes of not crying.

My mother gave me a hug and said, "What about expanding your dog-walking job? You should see about walking some of the other neighbors' dogs. And aren't you forgetting that you have two babysitting jobs lined up for this week?"

But I didn't want to be in the presence of my mom's optimism anymore. "It's just getting on my nerves that all I do is work, work, work, and it seems I'm getting nowhere!" My parents both laughed at that, which I really didn't appreciate.

Then, my mom finally started making some sense. "When I was in college and we needed money, my roommate and I scrounged our closets and drawers for stuff we didn't need anymore. Then we'd set up a card table and sell it. Like a flea-market boutique!"

"A yard sale," my father offered.

"A boutique," my mom said firmly.

❀ ❀ ❀

From that moment, Lily and I became "boutique" freaks. We cleared out our closets of old clothes and toys, then piled them all in my parents' garage until the sale we set for the following Saturday. Our parents even pitched in by "donating" stuff for us to sell. They didn't even ask for a cent, saying we were doing them a favor by getting rid of their junk. But that "junk" equaled cha-ching for us!

The day of the sale, I woke up at precisely 5:43 A.M. It was still kind of dark outside, but I didn't care. My dad helped me drag the big boxes from the garage, but I did most of the setting up myself. When I finished, I took a few steps back and looked, expecting to be amazed.

I was less than impressed. The table looked bare and, honestly, kind of depressing. The CD covers were dusty, and some were cracked. The hats, scarves, and mittens were all jumbled into one big pile. The stack of baskets was all uneven. Even the table where I had put the moneybox and calculator looked lame—it had a yellowish ring from my father's coffee cup.

All the time I spent digging that stuff up, and it looked like a box of junk had fallen off the back of a truck and landed in my yard. And it was already 7 A.M.—one hour until the sale was to start!

OK, Molly, think, I told myself. I had worked too hard to freak out now! *Why doesn't this look like a boutique?*

I went over to the box of my grandmother's things and pulled out a big flowery tablecloth and spread it across the table. Then I grabbed a bundle of plastic flowers and stuck it in a vase, turning the crack to face me. I tied one of my dad's funky ties around it and tied another around a big basket. Quickly, I took out all the mittens and pinned the matches together with safety pins. I neatly folded the scarves and put them with matching hats. Some even matched the mittens and gloves, so I put them together, too.

I sandwiched the CDs with cracked cases between ones that were in better condition, tied them up with ribbon and wrote "3-for-1!" on them. I organized the basket mess from biggest to smallest.

And I pulled out some of the best
stuff—a gumball machine, a
flowered picture frame, and a
Princess Amidala action
figure—for a display on
the table.

   I ran inside for
some cleaning spray,
a roll of paper towels,
and a damp sponge. Like
a crazy person, I wiped
everything down until the
sponge was dark brown and the towels were nearly gone—
everything looked much closer to new. I even swept the driveway
so no grass clippings or anything was on the path to my sale, and
tacked one of the hot-pink flyers Lily and I had made to a tree.

   As I walked back up the driveway and eyed my yard sale, it
looked different—almost pretty! My mother came from around
back, still in her robe but wearing her gardening clogs and gloves.
She was holding a small bouquet of flowers from her garden:
Daffodils, bright pink roses, black-eyed Susans, and two tall irises.
"For your boutique," she said, bleary-eyed but smiling, and she
stuck them in a secondhand vase.

Lily arrived around 8 A.M., bringing Min-Min along for good luck.
The day was a blur, and by 3 P.M. almost everything had been sold,
except for some of the CDs and a few little things. We had earned
$119.28, which, added to my $170, put us way over our goal!

   I wanted to turn cartwheels in the driveway, I was so happy.
But Lily was beat. "We've got enough," she said. "Let's close shop."

   "But our flyers say we'll be in business 'til four," I said. Even
with the little we had left, I didn't want anyone hauling themselves
to our sale for nothing.

   "But we have the money, even lots extra!" Lily said, sounding
a little bossy.

And then—probably because we were tired and hot and thirsty—we started to argue, not realizing Min-Min had slipped away. That is, not until Austin, of all people, skated up with Min-Min tucked under his arm. Austin kicked up his board and walked over to the table, holding Min-Min up for my inspection. "Is this your dog?"

Too nervous to respond, I shook my head and pointed to Lily. Austin looked at the stuff we had left, and then grabbed the Princess Amidala doll, which, surprisingly, no one had bought yet.

"This would be cool—I mean, for my sister," he said, blushing in a way that made him even cuter.

"It's, um, three dollars," I said.

"Cool," he said.

I opened the cash box as Austin pulled a $50 from his pocket. I stared at the bill. After a day of collecting ones and fives and nickels and quarters, it strangely looked like a lot of money.

Suddenly, I remembered I had totally forgotten about the $50 I had found a few months ago! It was so crazy! I had been so busy earning and saving, that the money I'd found had slipped my mind. Really, I hadn't needed to freak out as much as I had the other morning. But somehow, I was still really glad that I had.

I suddenly had a brainstorm. "We can't break that," I said, closing the cash box so he couldn't see inside. I smiled and began to carefully put the doll into a bag.

Lily gave me that 'what are you doing?' look. I gave her an 'I know what I'm doing' kick under the table.

Then, handing the $50 back to Austin, I said, "Just bring the three bucks to me tomorrow. At the pool."

"Cool," he said, flashing me that smile that could stop a comet. Austin fumbled a little as he put the doll into his messenger bag. Then, he pulled out his cell phone and waved it.

"Maybe I'll, you know, call you," Austin said, looking at me almost sideways as he turned it on. "Just to…um…confirm."

"Yeah, cool, give me a call. To confirm," I repeated, smiling the whole time.

But when he said, "What's your cell?" I started to laugh.

It was so funny. If I hadn't done all this stuff to get a cell, Austin probably would have never given me the time of day. But now, here he was, right in my front yard asking for my cell phone number. But, weirdly, now that I had the money, the cell phone didn't even matter so much.

"Just call my house. My mom confirms all my appointments," I joked.

"Cool," he said, and he programmed my home number into his phone.

Flush It and Forget It

JESSICA ZIEGLER

*Sometimes all you need to stop good friends from fighting
is to share one big ol' pizza pie.*

My best friend, Claire, was totally hyper in school all morning, like she had eaten a bag of sugar and guzzled a gallon of Diet Coke. I mean, even on her calmest days, Claire was pretty crazy—like a couple of weeks ago when she made up a cheer with me during homeroom for Mr. Scott, our band teacher, that went, "Mr. Scott is so hot, he'll never ever stop!" I know it doesn't really make sense, but when you sing it over and over again, until your biology teacher yells at you, it's kind of hysterical. But it seemed like, even for Claire, something was up.

We were sitting in Band during third period, and I was trying to figure out what was up with her. I knew she had a crush on Collin Hannon, so I thought maybe something had happened that she didn't tell me about yet. Then Claire passed me a note that had been folded like a million times in her signature way, with the last edge tucked in "to protect it from enemies," and it explained everything.

Dear Zelly,

You are _not_ my best friend. You never were my friend at all.

I wrote back:

Dear Claire,

What did I do?

She replied:

Nothing. I just never really liked you.

Claire smiled at me like everything was fine between us. I read the note again just to make sure. Her hurtful words still sat there on the page, and I was afraid I was going to lose it and get sick right there in front of everybody. Mr. Scott raised his baton and Claire placed her clarinet between her lips like a soldier might raise her weapon.

I wanted to hide Claire's letter behind some music on my stand, but when I began to do it, the little piece of paper was shaking in my hand. I didn't want anyone, especially Trish who sat right behind me, to see the evidence that proved my best friend hated me. I managed to unclench my fist and purposely dropped the sweaty note on the floor under my chair. I planned to hide it away during our next break. Maybe, by then, I wouldn't be shaking like a total freak. I looked over at Claire, who was relaxed and poised. She was the queen of concentration. Mr. Scott held out his arms to get everyone's attention. He would notice if I didn't at least pick the clarinet up.

I pictured him waving his arms for everyone to stop and then he'd taunt me with, "And Zelly, is there a reason you are too good to play with us today?"

Tears would stream down my face. Claire would laugh, her perfect white teeth shining in my face.

"Oh, my god!" she would scream as she turned to make sure Trish, the most popular girl in school, could see how stupid I looked.

The black plastic clarinet felt too light in my hand, as if I hadn't been carrying it around for the past three years. I wrapped my lips around my dry mouthpiece and pretended to play for an entire song. Claire knew I wasn't playing, but that was our secret for now. She hated me for getting first clarinet seat. She must have been happy to hear my silence.

Mr. Scott called a bathroom break and Claire ran over to Trish, in the second clarinet row, right behind me. I kept looking down at my music as if I were studying the section we had just played. I heard Claire's loud hyena laugh that teachers always were telling her to stop. Usually it was "Claire and Zelly! No side talking!" From now on, it would be Claire and Trish, best friends forever. Their whispers faded, and I finally felt safe enough to turn around. The first thing I saw was Claire's long finger, pointing toward me. Trish and her group giggled like popular people do. I slid down in my chair, shrinking to the size of the mole on Mr. Scott's left cheek.

I bent down to pick up the note that I had left under my chair, but I didn't feel it. I stuck my head down between my legs. It was gone. I knew who had taken it. Trish sat right behind me. Little Miss Perfect with her silky black hair and sparkled pink shirt that said "Goddess Power!" was obviously part of Claire's plan to cut me off from everyone. That must have been what was so funny. Tears threatened to spill out of my eyes. I looked up at the Band room ceiling, which I tried to think about in a very detailed way. The pattern could either be looked at as squares or as diamonds, depending on your point of view.

Mr. Scott got up on his little wooden platform that looked as if it might break into a thousand pieces one day from his increasingly round figure. Unfortunately for me, I knew where he fed that expanding body. I saw Mr. Scott every Tuesday night at Milo's, the local greasy pit of shame in our town. It was my mom's favorite place to embarrass me on a weekly basis, and Mr. Scott shared my mom's strange desire to eat there. Trish would never walk into a place like Milo's. Tonight, being a Tuesday night, meant I was going to be lucky enough to spend some extra quality time with Mr. Scott.

I managed to play the rest of the songs during practice, but when Mr. Scott dropped his arms and bellowed "Finale!" like he was a famous opera singer instead of a boring sixth grade music teacher, I shoved my clarinet into its case, not bothering to clean it or even to fit it properly into the plush blue cushions. I grabbed my music, letting one piece fly out of my grip as I stomped out of the room.

I dropped my clarinet in my locker, which usually I would never do without Claire. After Band every day, Claire always wants to wait until Collin Hannon's group walks by. Claire pretends to say something funny, and I, drawing from my years of acting training that I got from watching soap operas, laugh in a dramatic, yet believable way. After they pass, Claire and I always write a thought for the day on the "Claire & Zelly, Best Friends Forever" posters that are inside each of our locker doors. But not today.

I was finally able to catch Claire alone after English in the hallway. We stood only inches apart as we both looked into our lockers, but it felt like she was miles away. I imagined myself all alone, a return visitor on my way to the North Pole on Claire Airlines. I shivered from the icy wind. I gave her a couple moments to see if she might say something to me. She just continued putting books into her locker without looking my way.

Claire had sent me to the North Pole before, and I knew she wouldn't invite me to her popular party-land until she was good and ready. But I couldn't stand it—I *had* to talk to her. So I squeaked out, "Um, Claire, I mean, um, are you okay?"

I hoped her not talking to me was part of some complicated scheme against Becky, this girl who Claire always picks on. I had been hoping that Claire just hadn't had a chance to tell me about it yet. Instead, she slammed her locker door in my face and walked away without saying a word. The North Pole wasn't where I was anymore. I was on another planet entirely!

I tore down the sign that read, "Claire and Zelly—BFF!" from inside my locker door and walked out to the school yard where all the different groups of kids were hanging out before walking home. I waited in the school yard, hiding off behind a tree for awhile to see if Trish might walk by. I was desperate and thought maybe she would take pity on me. Even though she's the most popular girl in school, she's usually nice to everybody.

Trish walked out in her totally cool jean jacket that she had painted on the back in silver, "Indians Rock!" to announce to the world that she's cool enough to become an Indians high school cheerleader someday. Trish was too busy laughing hysterically with Claire to notice me. Claire hadn't mentioned that she wasn't taking the bus home today and she definitely didn't say anything about hanging out with Trish. The sun reflected off of Trish's shiny jacket and Claire's purple bag. They looked like two movie stars as they walked by.

That's when Michael Fanta, the lone tuba player in the band who hardly ever speaks to anyone, came up behind me as I hid behind the tree and yelled, "Zelly, Queen of the Underworld!"

Everyone stopped talking and turned my way, including Claire, who looked at me like I was a piece of gum she spat out last week. She walked over to me, leaving Trish waiting for her.

"Um, Zelly, get a life," she hissed, as if I already didn't feel bad enough. "We don't want you following us like a total loser."

I hadn't realized how obvious it was that I had been waiting for Trish. I looked behind Claire at Trish, who was pointing at my note  in her hand. Why did she need to torture me? She was mouthing something, and I was glad I couldn't make it out. I pushed past Claire and through the silent crowd. Everyone stared at me like I was their after-school entertainment. I put my head down and counted the cracks in the sidewalk as I walked, each step bringing me closer to home. Normally, after school, I would just walk across the street to my cousin Marcy's house—I normally had to go there until my mom was done with work. But luckily, my mom was off work and so I could walk farther away from all those staring eyes.

When I got home, my mother's boyfriend, Vince, was walking around my house with his big ugly hands and shiny bald spot, acting like he was doing us this big favor, taking us out to Milo's. He told me to "dress for success". What was that about? Milo's is a totally cruddy place. It's really a takeout pizza place with some booths that only loser people sit in. Going to Milo's for takeout pizza is actually a very cool thing to do in my town, but for the sit-in dinners, they cook gross things like liver and onions (my mother's favorite, even though she's a "vegetarian"—figure that one out). The only person we've ever run into who actually sits in the booths there is Mr. Scott, the music teacher. My mom's boyfriend is the music teacher from the next town. Why are music teachers so weird, anyway?

My mom sent me upstairs to change, and I just looked in the mirror at myself for like ten minutes without doing anything. It was as if for the first time I was noticing my different body parts, my arms, my legs, my head, and that they didn't really fit together like

Trish or Claire's did. My full name is Zeferella Marie March-McFarland. It doesn't get much stranger than that.

My mom knocked on my door, calling, "Let's go, sweetie!"

She didn't even notice when I came out wearing the same outfit I had worn to school.

The owners of Milo's, Milo and Rose, greeted us when we walked in the door. Rose was the *only* good reason to go to Milo's. Even if everything else seemed embarrassing about that place, a good hug from Rose made it all go away. I didn't mind that some of the flour from Rose's apron smudged onto my black jeans when she pulled me in for a "Ciao Bella!" hug.

"Oh, Zelly, my dear. Why the sad face?" Rose asked.

My mom and Vince had already found a big red booth in the center of the restaurant so we could be on display like a circus act.

"Nothing," I muttered.

"Oh no, I know you better than that. What's wrong?" she said.

"I dunno," I practically whispered.

"I'll be watching you," Rose said in her loving way. I was looking forward to following her into the kitchen at the end of our meal, like I always do, so she could fry up her lace cookies that she makes just for me.

My mom and Vince had already scooted into one side, leaving me all alone on the other. I sat down. I didn't want to think of them holding hands under the table, but, once I thought of it, I couldn't get it out of my head.

"What are you going to have, honey?" my mom asked, totally ignoring the fact that a restaurant's cook had shown more concern for my sad mood than she had.

I don't know why my mom asks me this question every time we're at Milo's, and why I then ask her what she's going to have. I always order the pizza, and my mom always has liver and onions. Vince is the wild card, playing the whole menu out over time, and sometimes he just leaves it to Rose to decide.

Mr. Scott walked in as Rose placed "the house special Shirley Temple just for the sweet girl" in front of me. My mom called, "Matt, come and sit with us." My mom says that Mr. Scott doesn't have anyone, and we should be nice to him. I think I'm nice enough every day during Band, and there is no need to expand that into my non-school hours. Mr. Scott pretended he was actually considering turning us down, forcing my mom to use her next line, "Oh, come on, Matt. Zelly saved you a seat." She always says that—and it absolutely kills me every time.

Just when I thought life couldn't get any worse, Claire, Trish, and Trish's mom walked in the door and headed for the takeout counter. Getting pizza as takeout from Milo's is one thing, but eating there in a booth with your mom's boyfriend and your Band teacher is a whole different animal. I was sure this would make Claire and Trish hate me forever. I slid as low as possible under the table, and I watched them look up at the menu on the wall. Trish's mom paid Rose and handed the pizza to Trish. The three of them turned back around. Trish and Claire were laughing about something, obviously dying to get away from the embarrassing booth dwellers like me.

Just as Claire's hand was on the door, Trish's mom innocently declared, "Oh, look, girls. It's Zelly!"

I looked at my table of losers and that was all the evidence I needed to know that I was destined to become a music teacher someday. Trish smiled at me. She nudged Claire, who also smiled, but I could tell she was using her fake smile for the parents. My mom stood and called Trish's mom by her first name, hugging her like they were best friends, which they're totally not. I hoped Trish's mom didn't think my mom was a total loser. Trish's mom looked amazing in a pair of fitted white pedal pushers and a pink T-shirt. She and Trish had the exact same deep black hair, and it wasn't like a weird mother/daughter thing. They just looked cool. Then, my mom introduced Vince to Trish's mom.

Trish's mom smiled and said, "Oh you have a wonderful man,

here. Don't let him get away!" to my mom. She continued, "Good to see you, Mr. Scott."

"It's Matt. Call me Matt," Mr. Scott abruptly spit out, his face turning bright red.

All this time, Trish was smiling at me like she was happy to see me, like she hadn't just stolen my best friend.

"Hey, girls," Trish's mom suddenly declared. "Why don't we stay? Rose, can we eat our pizza here?"

"Wonderful!" Rose announced, running towards the kitchen.

Trish's mom turned to Mr. Scott and whispered, "I've never eaten here before." Of course she hadn't ever sat in the booths at Milo's. She had a life! Rose ran over with three plates and called Johnny, their son, to take a drink order.

"Zelly, come over here with your friends," Rose said.

Rose put out plates for Trish, Claire, and me at the booth across from the adults. Rose and Trish smiled at each other. Rose seemed to give Claire a scolding look. Rose had our situation figured out in two seconds. She was like a fortune-teller.

Trish said, "Zelly, sit next to me," as she slid into the booth Rose had laid out for us.

Mr. Scott got up to let me out. After I moved, he bowed to Trish's mom. He wore a hat of sweat, and his eyes were opened a little too wide, but Trish's mom didn't seem to mind at all. She sat down at the music-teacher convention.

Claire looked across the table at me, still wearing her fake for-parents-only smile. But then, Trish turned to me.

"I have to go to the bathroom. Want to come, Zelly?" Trish asked me. Trish was being too nice. I didn't trust it.

I said, "No, that's okay."

"C'mon. Please," Trish pleaded.

"I'll go," Claire announced.

Claire sat up very straight in her seat. I could tell that she was insulted that Trish hadn't asked her to go to the bathroom with her.

"No, that's okay. Zelly's coming," Trish said, as she pushed me out of the seat.

Claire looked at me like I had slapped her. Her top lip curled over her big perfect teeth, changing her into a chipmunk rather than the shark she had been earlier that day.

"Yes. I'll keep your friend here busy!" Rose said, sitting down next to Claire, blocking her from following us.

I don't know why I followed Trish through the long line of booths toward the sign that said, "Signoras." I had little hope that this would turn out all right. Trish closed the door behind us and dug her hand into the pocket of her low-waist jeans. She pulled out a crumpled piece of paper.

"I've been trying to give this to you all day," she revealed. I opened it. It was the horrible note she had stolen from me during Band. "I saw you drop it," she said, "Let's keep this our secret. Claire doesn't know I've even seen it."

I found this hard to believe. I had seen them laughing at me during class.

"You're not best friends?" I asked.

"Me and Claire? No. Don't worry, Zelly. Claire will get over it," Trish said.

I started replaying my horrible day in my mind, going over all the times that I thought Trish was laughing at me and the scenes started to change. I realized that each time I had been convinced that Trish was torturing me, she was really trying to help. Claire, on the other hand, was as mean as she had always been, willing to turn on me in an instant.

Trish looked at herself in the mirror. She was so lucky. She never had to worry about anything. Her shirt was flowered and fitted to her body—far too stylish for a pizza place. She caught my eye in the mirror. I was still holding the note, like a big fool.

"Hey, let's flush it!" Trish exclaimed. She walked over to a stall and waved me to her. "Come on. Throw it in," she encouraged. I let it fall from my hand. It hit the edge of the seat and plunged into the water. Trish stepped on the handle and we watched the tiny letter swirl around and then disappear. "Flush it and forget it," Trish announced.

"Hey! What are you two up to?" Claire interrupted.

She had opened the door while we were focused on saying goodbye to the worst note I've ever gotten. She had that I'm-totally-relaxed-but-not-really tone to her voice.

"Nothing, girlfriend," Trish said.

"Hey," Claire murmured.

She was looking right at me. Trish was washing her hands.

"Hey," I replied.

"Where's Marcy?" Claire asked, in an annoyed tone. Marcy was my cousin who was in junior high, where we would be next year. We had become close recently, since I had to go over to her house after school a lot.

"I don't know. Why?" I replied, starting to think of the reason that Claire might have written the note to me.

"I just thought. You two are like twins. Always together," she said, looking down at the cracked linoleum.

Marcy was pretty and popular, but she was my cousin, and I could tell she wasn't totally happy that she had to hang out with me after school when I went to her house. Claire obviously hadn't picked up on that fact.

"Not really," I said, "I'm just her cousin."

Claire and I locked eyes for a minute, long enough for me to know that we were thinking the same thing. Marcy wasn't in the picture the way Claire thought, and I still wanted Claire as my best friend. I could tell from the growing smile on her face that she was over it, knowing she hadn't been replaced by my cousin. What she didn't know, though, was that I was over it, too. I mean, Claire was my best friend, even if she was an idiot at times. She puffed out her lip into her "angry look" and then she crossed her eyes and started to laugh. That was Claire's way of telling me she was sorry, and then we all started to laugh.

We walked back to the table, Claire, then me, then Trish. Rose was waiting for us.

"You girls, come back with me. Into the kitchen," she said.

The mothers and music teachers were enjoying themselves too much to even notice us. Claire started whispering our cheer for Mr. Scott into my ear, as we followed Rose and Trish into the kitchen for her famous lace cookies. Rose grabbed a long wooden spoon and mixed the pale batter.

"Hand me the mold, please, Zelly," she said as she pointed to the tarnished metal snowflake mold with a long handle which lay on the counter. She took the snowflake from me and plunged it into the batter.

"You got to get it just right," Rose said. She motioned for Trish and Claire to clear the way, and she held the dripping snowflake above the bowl, and then swung it over to a pot on the stove. She dropped the snowflake into the pot. Claire jumped back at the sound of the sizzling oil. I took her hand and pulled her back toward the giant old stove where I always waited for my cookies. Rose let the cookie separate from the metal mold and gently rise to the top. She went back to the batter twice more. When all three snowflakes were golden and waiting at the top of the liquid, Rose handed me the metal net, and I spooned them out, one by one, and placed them carefully onto a plate that Rose had covered with paper towels. Rose handed Claire the finishing touch, a bag of powdered sugar. Trish took a pinch and sprinkled it over the cookies. We greedily ate our three snowflakes and laughed at our messy hands and faces.

Rose just smiled.

The Truth About the Queen B

Emilie Le Beau

Brianna St. Ives is rich, beautiful, and hangs out
with movie stars on a regular basis. When she visits
her ordinary old pen-pal, Nora, will Nora's plain-Jane life
be able to keep Brianna entertained?

"Oh, no," I said, putting down the letter. "She's coming." I looked down at my bulldog, Barney. He wagged his tail. "No Barn," I said. "This is not good."

For the last three months, I've been the forced pen pal to Brianna St. Ives of Malibu, California. As if the required-for-all-seventh-graders "Health and Family" class wasn't lame enough, we were given pen pals.

And not just a pen pal, but a real-deal pen pal. No phones, no e-mail, only pen and paper. Our teacher said it would "slow the process down." Whatever that means. All I know is I'm supposed to write a three-page essay on Queen Brianna and her life as Malibu Barbie. I have to compare her life in California to my life in Chicago.

Compare our lives? We have *nothing* in common. Brianna says everything I do is "cute" or "sweet." I live with my mom and my little sister. (Cute! Letter two.) My dad's job moved him to Cincinnati a few months ago, so we only get to seem him on weekends. It's super hard on us, especially my mom. She really misses my dad a lot. (Oh, that's so sweet. Letter three.) Even my name, Nora, is "cute."

And Brianna? Well, nothing she does is "cute" or "sweet." Brianna says she's totally sophisticated. She lives with her mom, but her dad lives just three miles away and takes her to movie premieres and introduces her to celebrities. She says she's met Mandy Moore, Ashton Kutcher, and my all-time fave, Kirstin Dunst.

Brianna loves, loves, loves to shop and even has a computer in her room. When she can't make it to the mall, she just shops online. Must be nice. Besides shopping, Brianna says she loves to ride her horse on the beach. Don't we all?

The worst part about Brianna? She's coming to Chicago and wants to see me! I can barely handle Brianna on paper, but Brianna in person? Ugh, no thanks.

"My dad has a meeting in Chicago," she wrote. *"Let's do lunch."*

I put the letter back in the envelope and groaned. "Great, just great," I told Barney. He looked up at me with that hungry look.

"Fine, here," I said, dropping the purple envelope. It floated slowly to the ground. Barney picked it up with his mouth and went running into the kitchen.

In study hall the next day, I spent my last period of the day trying to draft my Brianna essay. "All about the Queen B" I wrote on the top of the paper before I scratched it out. I knew I could never call her the nickname I had made up. Even though it fits. In her fourth letter, Brianna wrote that my dress I had earlier described to her for my back-to-school dance sounded "simple." It was glittery, red, and gorgeous. Far from simple! I wanted to tell her the dress was really pretty and no one wore anything like it. I even thought about sending her a picture of me dancing with my friend Carlos—he's super cute.

My mom told me I don't need to defend myself when I know the truth. She said I knew my dress was nice so I shouldn't waste my time trying to justify it to Brianna. But it was hard not saying something, and just letting it go.

I saved the dress letter because I thought I might need to bring it up in my paper. Of the twelve letters Brianna had written, two were so braggy that I had fed them to Barney. Another time, she wrote about how her mom's house was mansion-big and she couldn't imagine not having her own bathroom. It made me feel bad about my house, so I gave the letter to my little sister. She shredded it and used it as liner in her hamster cage. I had a huge sense of satisfaction from knowing Mr. Squeakers was tromping all over her letter.

I looked at the clock (five minutes until the bell) and then out the window at the falling snow. We already had a big snowfall this winter and now they were predicting another eight inches. It was like living in a snow globe. Letter five from the Queen B bragged about all the California sunshine. *"I heard on television that Chicago hasn't seen sunlight in twenty-four days. Wow, that's depressing. I would totally hate my life if I hadn't seen the sun in twenty-four days."*

The bell rang and I stood up to pull on my coat. We're not supposed to bring our coats to class, but Carlos offered to walk me home and I didn't want him to wait while I hiked up to my fourth-floor locker and back. Carlos was already doing me a big favor by keeping me company and then racing back to school for his basketball practice.

"Hey you," he said as I walked up to his locker. "Ready to go?"

"Yup!" I answered cheerfully.

We headed out the double doors and into snowy streets. Carlos started our usual snowy-day routine: He walks first to stomp out a little path and I follow. He says he doesn't want me to get my jeans wet and I always feel bad when I see his jeans caked with snow.

"Do you baby-sit tonight?" Carlos asked, stomping out a few steps. He stopped and waited for me to catch up.

"Nope," I called. "I'm working on my pen-pal paper."

"I hated that assignment," Carlos said, bending down to pick snow out of his shoe. I'm sure Brianna would freak if she had to walk six blocks home in the snow. The only other option is the bus, and I'd rather walk with Carlos. I had told Brianna about Carlos and how he's an eighth grader. She didn't mention him in her next letter, so I guess it just bored her.

"It's not *that* bad," I replied. "I just wish I didn't have to meet her."

Carlos continued stomping out a fresh path. "Just skip it, Nora," he said. "You don't have to meet her to write a good paper."

Skip it. I didn't think I could do that. It seemed so mean.

"I don't know, Carlos," I said, stepping carefully in his

footprints. "I don't think I could just turn her down."

"What's worse? Turning her down or dealing with the Queen B for a full afternoon?"

"I don't know," I answered truthfully. "I feel I'd know her better if we met. Maybe I'd write a better paper."

We walked a few blocks and turned onto my street. I hoped Carlos wouldn't be late because of me. He stomped his feet on the ground to warm them up. "So," he asked. "When are you supposed to meet her?"

"Saturday," I groaned. It was just three days away. "She wants me to meet her at her hotel."

Carlos and I walked up to my house. We stopped in front of the steps and Carlos adjusted his backpack. "I don't have a basketball game on Saturday. I can walk with you to the train station, if you want."

"Really?" I asked. "You'd do that?"

"Sure," he said, smiling. "Keep you company."

"You're the best," I told him.

Soon, it was Saturday afternoon and I was a wreck. Nothing was following my plan. I gave Barney a bath around 10 A.M. and put a cute paper ribbon around his neck. He ate the ribbon and then yakked it all over the dining room floor. I spent more time cleaning up doggy barf than I did getting ready. When Carlos showed up at noon, my hair was still wet and I had no time for anything but a bit of lip gloss.

"You look really nice," Carlos assured me. "I like it when you wear your hair wavy."

I patted the frizz ball that was supposed to be my hair. "You mean frizzy."

"Oh stop," Carlos said sweetly. "You look nice."

I grabbed my coat and followed Carlos down the steps. We walked about two blocks and then my hands felt really cold. As I reached into my pocket for my gloves, I realized I still had on the nail polish I let my sister paint on the night before.

"Oh, no," I moaned.

"What?" Carlos asked.

I held up my hands and revealed the world's ugliest manicure. Three of my fingers were painted yellow, three were green, and four had polka dots.

"I baby-sat my sister last night and let her do my nails. I totally forgot to take it off this morning."

"Do you want to run back and take it off?" Carlos asked, his breath making clouds in the cold air.

"I'm out of nail polish remover. That's another thing I was supposed to do this morning. Besides, I don't want to be late."

Carlos thought for a moment. "Can you pick it off?"

I tried to pick off a polka dot but I couldn't work off a good chip. "No," I cried. "It's too fresh."

Carlos took his back pack off and rummaged through the pockets. He stood up and handed me a red permanent marker.

"Always prepared," he said proudly, offering me the marker.

"What should I do with this?" I asked. "Write 'Idiot' on my forehead?"

Carlos laughed. "No, just use it to cover your nail polish. You know, color your nails with marker."

I shrugged and took off the cap. "I might as well give it a try," I said and began coloring.

By the time I walked up to the hotel, I smelled like a permanent marker. But my nails looked slightly better, at least they were almost one color. You couldn't see the polka dots anymore, so I considered it an improvement.

I walked on the sidewalk around the hotel's circular drive and I felt a clenching feeling in my stomach. It was Queen B time and I didn't know what to expect. I didn't even know why I was there.

I crossed through a row of yellow taxis and walked in the hotel on a thick red carpet. The hotel was so glamorous, I felt like I didn't belong with my wet hair and marker manicure. The lobby was incredible. The floors were black marble and there was a large fountain in the middle of the room. I walked over to the elevators and pressed the golden 'up' button.

I rode up the elevator and wandered down the hall to room 1258. I ran my fingers through my waves, attempting to de-frizz, and knocked on the door. No response—just the sounds of a TV playing loudly. I knocked again and finally heard the lock being undone.

The door swung open.

"Brianna?" I asked, surprised that the girl in front of me was Brianna. I thought Brianna would be a Hilary Duff look-a-like—that's totally how she described herself in her first letter. She said she was always getting mistaken for Hilary Duff.

But the girl in front of me didn't look anything like Hilary. She looked really tired and I couldn't be sure if her outfit was pajamas or real clothes.

"You must be Nora," Brianna said with a half smile, holding the door open.

"Hi!" I said brightly, walking into a way huge hotel room. "It's really nice to meet you."

"You too," Brianna said. "Hey, you can put your coat on the back of the chair."

I followed Brianna through an entryway and into a dining room. I didn't even know hotels had dining rooms! Sometimes, I'd travel to Cincinnati for the weekend if my dad was too busy to come home. We'd just stay in dinky motels, the type where an ice machine is big-time luxury.

I left my coat on the chair and followed Brianna into the living room. She picked up the TV remote and plopped down on the couch. "Do you like *TRL*?" she asked.

"What's that?" I asked, sitting in a chair next to the couch.

"You know, the video countdown on MTV."

"Oh yeah," I said, feeling stupid. "We don't have cable so I don't really watch a lot of TV."

"What!?" Brianna shrieked like I was an idiot. "How can you not have cable? I'd die without cable!"

I shrugged. "My mom says all we'd do is rot in front of the TV if we had cable."

Brianna raised her eyebrows. "Stinks to be you," she said, flipping through the channels.

Brianna flipped through the channels until she landed on *America's Funniest Home Videos*. "I love this show," she sighed. "Do you watch it?"

"Sometimes," I said, just to be nice, even though it wasn't true. "It's pretty funny."

Brianna kept watching and totally cracked up when a baby fell face first into his birthday cake. I scanned my eyes around the room and got a good look at the place. The suite was really nice, the furniture was soft, and the carpet was a pretty dark red. But everything seemed really messy. There were potato chip bags all over the coffee table, a stash of magazines on the love seat, and a bunch of empty soda cans on the ground.

Even Brianna looked a little messy. She was wearing pink velour pants and a matching sweatshirt. There was a huge yellow stain on the right leg and a blue stain on the front pocket. Her hair was pulled up into a ponytail and she looked like she hadn't showered.

Brianna picked through the pile of mess on the coffee table and pulled out a bag of Cheetos. "Want some?" she asked, popping a few in her mouth.

"Um, no thanks," I answered, watching her wipe cheesy fingers on her pants.

Brianna picked up the remote and began flipping through the channels again. She landed on a rerun of *Full House* and I began to think Brianna was a huge TV fan.

"Have you seen much of Chicago?" I asked.

Brianna laughed. "Not too much. My dad's been busy with meetings and stuff."

I could understand about her dad being busy with work. I would feel bad if she came all this way and didn't get to see anything good. "If you want, we can take a walk down Michigan Avenue."

Brianna looked up from the TV. "Oh, thanks but my dad said he would take me later."

I smiled. "That's cool. I think you'll have fun."

Brianna nodded, and flipped to *Jeopardy!* "I love it when they have the teen tournament," she said.

I was about to tell Brianna how my uncle once tried out for *Jeopardy!* when her dad walked in. He was wearing a pair of jeans and a heavy winter jacket. It didn't look like he had come from a meeting.

"Hey B," he said, giving Brianna a kiss on the forehead. I thought of my private nickname for her, The Queen B, and tried not to giggle.

Brianna's dad walked over to greet me and I stood up. "You must be Beverly's friend," he said, shaking my hand.

Beverly? Who was Beverly? I thought. I just smiled and nodded. "Nice to meet you Mr. St. Ives."

Brianna's dad gave me a confused look. "Who is St. Ives?"

I felt confused. "Who is Beverly?"

Brianna's dad pointed at her. "My daughter."

"You mean Brianna?" I asked.

Mr. St. Ives sighed and looked at Brianna. "Beverly," he said sternly, "you have to stop this nonsense."

Brianna shrugged. "Sorry," she mumbled.

Brianna's dad gave me an embarrassed look. "I'm John Iverston. And this is my daughter, Beverly."

I looked at Brianna (Beverly?). She was watching TV, ignoring everything around her. I didn't know what to say, so I just introduced myself. "I'm Nora Victoria," I told him and we shook hands again.

"Victoria? Is that your last name? That's different."

I nodded. "Yup. My great-grandfather came to Chicago in the late 1800s from England and renamed himself after the Queen."

"Really?" Brianna piped up from the couch. "Why?"

I love telling the story about my last name. "My great-grandfather left England because he didn't like the Queen. He took her name just to be bratty, just to make her name seem more common. Less royal."

Brianna reached for the Cheetos bag again. "That's so cool," she said. "I've always wondered why you had a girl's name for a last name."

I sat back down in the chair and Mr. Iverston cleared some junk off the couch and sat next to Brianna. "I think my real family name is actually Cooper," I said.

Beverly popped a few more Cheetos in her mouth. "Victoria is so cool."

Mr. Iverston rolled his eyes. "Don't get any ideas Beverly. Next thing we know you'll be Beverly Victoria."

Beverly gave her dad a sneer and picked up the remote again, turning to MTV and some music video. Her dad watched a few seconds and gave the TV a dirty look. "Do you like music videos?" he asked me.

"We don't have cable so I don't really see too many."

"This one," Mr. Iverston smirked, pointing at Beverly, "watches TV all day long."

"That's not true," Beverly shot back, flipping to a news report and watching the weather update on mute. "I do other things."

We were silent for a minute. Mr. Iverston seemed bored, and I couldn't believe all that I had heard. So Brianna St. Ives is really Beverly Iverston and her life as Malibu Barbie is more like TV Addict Barbie? I wasn't sure if I was mad at her for lying to me or relieved that she wasn't as picture-perfect as she seemed in her letters.

"How's your horse?" I asked Beverly, just trying to make conversation.

"Horse?" Mr. Iverston repeated. "You have a horse now?"

Mr. Iverston sighed, accidentally kicking over one of the empty soda cans. He picked it up and set it on the table.

"No," Beverly lied. "I never said I had a horse."

"I hope not," her dad said with a frown. He stood up. "I'm going to see how Lisa is coming along."

Mr. Iverston walked out of the living room and into another room I couldn't see. Beverly and I didn't really say anything to each other. She started watching a rerun of *That '70s Show* and I picked at my marker manicure.

Mr. Iverston walked back into the room with a brunette woman already bundled up in a hat and scarf. "Hi Bev!" she said brightly.

"Hey Lisa," Beverly called over her shoulder, sounding bored.

Lisa seemed nice. "We're going to see Michigan Avenue. Do you girls want to come?"

Beverly answered quickly. "No thanks."

Mr. Iverston frowned. "Beverly, I brought you all the way to Chicago and all you want to do is watch TV. You can watch TV at home."

"Just go with Lisa," Beverly answered sourly. Everyone was silent for a moment. I was so surprised. I could never talk like that to my parents. I'd be grounded from the phone for life!

But I guess Beverly could say whatever she wanted to her dad. Mr. Iverston just buttoned his jacket, waved goodbye to me, and left with a disgusted look on his face. Beverly kept watching TV. I think maybe her feelings were hurt because her dad was going out with Lisa and not her.

"I hate her," Beverly mumbled, her eyes glued to the TV.

"Who?" I asked, thinking she meant one of the characters on the show.

"Lisa," she growled.

"Oh." I answered. "Is she a friend of your dad's?"

Beverly sighed. "She's his new girlfriend. She *had* to come to Chicago, so here we are. No offense, but I would have been happy to stay home."

Great, I thought. *Another lie.* They were in Chicago because Lisa wanted to sightsee, not because her dad had some fancy lunch. It was just another thing I wish Beverly could have been honest about.

Beverly giggled at something Ashton Kutcher said on TV. It dawned on me that Beverly had probably never met Ashton Kutcher or any of those other celebrities. And she probably didn't shop online from her very own computer. I bet her house wasn't five stories tall, either.

Beverly was a big-time liar in her letters, but didn't really seem to have anything to say in person. It was no wonder—all she did was watch TV. I'm sure she was watching TV before I came and would keep watching after I left.

I stood up. "I should get going," I told her.

"That's cool," Beverly said, putting the TV on mute. She followed me out of the living room and into the dining room.

I pulled my arms through my coat. "Thanks for inviting me to hang out," I told her.

"Yeah!" Beverly said brightly. "I had a lot of fun."

Beverly unlocked the door and I stepped into the hallway. I didn't know what to say. Beverly and I had written our twelve letters, and we weren't required to write each other anymore. So what now?

"See you later," Beverly said.

"Yeah," I said cheerfully. "Have a safe trip home."

Beverly smiled and shut the door. I stood in the hallway alone and dug through my purse for train money. Within a few moments, I could hear the TV blaring again.

Something just seemed wrong and I didn't feel right not trying to fix it. I stood outside the door and took a deep breath. I knocked on the door again. I wondered if Beverly could hear me over the TV.

A minute later, I heard the sound of the lock being undone.

Beverly opened the door. "Did you forget something?" she asked.

"No," I said truthfully. "I just wanted to tell you something."

Beverly didn't open the door for me to come in. She was probably in the middle of a new show. I'd have to say my piece quickly so she could get back before the commercial was over.

"Umm..." I said nervously. Beverly raised an eyebrow. "Umm... You know, you didn't have to lie to me about all that stuff."

Beverly gave me an oh-well shrug.

"I don't know what to write for my school paper now, since everything you said was a lie."

Beverly sighed. "Just make something up."

"I can't do that," I said, my voice sounding nervous.

I could hear the sound of people clapping coming from the TV. Beverly looked over her shoulder and then back at me. "I gotta go, *Wheel of Fortune* is on. See you."

I stood stunned, as Beverly shut the door and did the lock. Make something up? Why would I want to do that? Maybe Beverly was into bending the truth but it didn't feel right to me. I rode down the elevator and walked through the marble lobby, grateful to be going home. I walked on the slushy sidewalk to the train station, trying to understand what had happened.

I thought about Beverly in front of the TV alone and felt sorry for her. Why a fake name? A fake life? I found a seat on the train and thought the truth about the Queen B was that there wasn't a lot of truth. Just a whole lot of lies.

I'm not sure why Beverly invited me to the hotel if she knew all her lies would get busted. Maybe she lied so much that it was all beginning to seem real. I leaned my head against the window and felt the cold.

I finally knew what I was going to write about in my paper.

I was going to have to explain how Beverly had lied about her life in California. Most of the stuff she had said wasn't true, and I would have had no way of knowing unless I had met her. I guess we all could have been anyone we wanted with our pen pals. Most pen pals never meet and won't know whether you're really head cheerleader or swim team captain. We could have been anyone we wanted—and Beverly wanted to be someone else.

My teacher wanted us to compare our lives with our pen pals' lives across the country. There wasn't much to compare between Beverly and I, only differences to point out. Beverly could have been herself, but that must have not seemed good enough.

The conductor called my stop and I stood up as the train doors opened. I stomped through the snow and felt glad to be going home. Even though it means no cable, no computer, no shopping sprees or celebrity lunches. Just a few good friends like Carlos and a paper-chewing dog.

The Magic Club

HEATHER ST. CLAIR CROSS

Not only can Jaclyn predict the future, she can cause people to get sick. Spencer's got to find some magic powers of her own—and fast!

It was Jaclyn's idea to form The Magic Club. Jaclyn had all the ideas. If someone else came up with an idea, she would make changes and then claim it was hers. Fourth grade was the first year I'd been in Jaclyn's class, but by the end of the opening week, I'd learned that Jaclyn has the best ideas. She knew things that none of us had heard of, and even though our teacher, Miss Swanson, seemed nice enough, we knew that everything important in school happened outside class time.

"There are only three rules," Jaclyn told us at recess the first day. "One: Everything that happens in The Magic Club is secret. If you repeat anything to *anyone*—your parents, our teacher, *anyone*—you'll be kicked out, and all the other girls will cast spells on you to make bad stuff happen."

"How are they going to do that?" asked Lela, doubtfully. Lela was the shortest fourth-grade girl, but, next to Jaclyn, she was the bossiest. I'd been in Lela's class since second grade, and was glad to see someone like Jaclyn put her in her place.

Jaclyn narrowed her eyes at Lela and spoke quietly. "That's what The Magic Club is about, Lela, learning magic spells and practicing them. I know lots of spells, and if you're nice, I'll teach them to you."

We giggled. We'd all been reading *Harry Potter*, but that didn't mean we thought real magic existed. Lela flipped her hair behind her ears and stuck her nose in the air. "Oh yeah?" she said. "Well if you're so smart, why don't you just show us, then? Why don't you make our teacher, Miss Swanson, disappear?" She gestured to me with her thumb.

I laughed nervously. "Come on, you guys," I said. "Let's just have fun." A couple of other girls murmured in agreement.

"No," said Jaclyn. "I'm not having anyone call me a liar." I began to protest that no one had called her anything, but Jaclyn cut me off. "Look over there," she said, pointing to a group of boys playing handball. "I'll cast a spell to get them in trouble. Watch." She fixed Lela with an angry stare, then closed her eyes and mumbled something. We couldn't understand what she was saying, but she continued to whisper fiercely and make small movements with her hands.

Lela sighed heavily. "You guys, this is so dumb." She stood up from the pavement and put her hands on her hips. "Let's go." A few girls glanced uneasily from Lela to Jaclyn and across at the boys. Then it happened. One of the boys dove for the handball and knocked another boy over. Before we knew it, they were wrestling on the ground. Then, Miss Swanson appeared and pulled them apart, scolding. We turned to Jaclyn, our mouths open. She sat cross-legged, her hands folded, a placid smile on her face.

"See," she said. "Now you know."

Jaclyn explained the last two rules of The Magic Club: 1) You would get a number to describe your level of magic power, and 2) You had to obey anyone with a higher number than yours. Anyone who broke the rules would get a bad spell cast on her.

I was lucky; I was made a five. Jaclyn, of course, was the only six. Most of the girls were fours, and Lela was made a three. The only other five was Jaclyn's longtime friend Claire. I wasn't sure why Jaclyn had made me a five when she hardly knew me, but maybe she could tell that I had strong magic potential inside me. Or maybe she liked the fact that I tried to shut Lela up. Whatever the reason, it meant that Jaclyn, Claire, and I could decide what to play at recess and the other girls had to go along with us. We got to go first in the lunch line, and if another girl was sitting in the bean-bag chair during free reading, we could kick her out and sit there ourselves.

Jaclyn rarely spoke to Lela and never gave her a direct order. Instead, she would ask me or Claire to tell her what to do. At recess, there were usually two groups for games. If Jaclyn was happy with you that day, you got to play in her group. If she was mad at you, you had to play with Lela. Some days, she would make three groups, and no one was allowed to play with Lela.

We read a lot of books together about wizards, sorceresses, and spells. At home, I even found a website about magic tools like wands and amulets. After a while, Jaclyn taught us a couple of basic spells, like how to make a boy not sit at your table. None of us was very good at getting our spells to work, and if we did, it seemed like a coincidence.

"That's because your magic powers aren't very strong," Jaclyn told us. "But they're like a muscle. Keep practicing, and you'll get better."

I finally succeeded in casting a spell the day after our first multiplication test. Jaclyn had taught us a spell for getting good test scores. The night after the test, you had to buy a pint of Ben & Jerry's Super Fudge Chunk ice cream, with your own money, then go home, scoop it out into a bowl, and let it all melt. Once it had melted, you had to say the magic spell (your full name plus the score you wanted) six times, with concentration. Then you had to pour the melted ice cream down the drain, *without eating a bite or even licking the spoon.* I followed the spell meticulously and spoke the words with every ounce of my magic powers. The next morning, during Math, Miss Swanson passed back our tests. Mine said 100%.

Of course, Jaclyn got 100%, too, but she made a big deal out of congratulating me on my powers. At recess, she passed out Skittles to all the girls in our group, which was everyone but Lela. We got one Skittle for each number of our powers. Because I'd done so well on my spell, she gave me six, but she was careful to point out that this didn't actually make me a six.

"Keep practicing, and you might get there," she said, patting me on the back.

Jaclyn's powers seemed limitless. Miss Swanson was strict about homework, but whenever Jaclyn didn't have hers with her, she would just cast a spell on our teacher and say, "I was busy last night." Miss Swanson would stare at her, shocked, but Jaclyn got away with it. Jaclyn could keep the boys away, or, if she wanted, she could get them to do things for her, like put away her spelling book. She got all hundreds on the weekly multiplication tests, she could predict what we were going to have for lunch, and she made

Lela get a big pimple right on her nose.

Even though I didn't like Lela, I started to feel a little sorry for her. She began spending recess in the bathroom and returning near the end, her eyes red. Jaclyn soon discovered this and, to keep Miss Swanson from getting suspicious and thinking we were excluding Lela, Jaclyn made Lela sit on the steps at recess and memorize a passage from one of her magic books. It took Lela over a week, but finally she recited the whole passage for us while Claire followed along to make sure she didn't make any mistakes. We all applauded when she finished, and even Jaclyn smiled. For a few days, she even let Lela play in her group.

The Friday before Halloween, Lela missed school. She missed the next Monday, too, and when Claire asked Miss Swanson if Lela was sick, Miss Swanson frowned and said she wasn't. Jaclyn got that knowing look on her face, so at recess we all swarmed around her.

"I'm not saying anything," she told us.

"Oh, come on, Jac," Claire pleaded. "You know something. I can tell you do!"

"I might or I might not," Jaclyn said. "But you'll all see soon enough."

We had to wait until Lela returned to school the next day to find out anything.

"Her grandfather is really sick," Claire whispered to me, just before Reading.

Suddenly, I felt sick. "Was he sick before?" I asked.

"I don't think so. She's really upset." We both turned to Jaclyn, but she had her hand up and was answering Miss Swanson's first question. Halfway through Reading, Lela went to the bathroom and didn't come back. At recess, there was still no sign of her, and Claire said she was probably talking to the school counselor. When Jaclyn arrived in the courtyard, we rushed to her.

"Omigod!" we cried. "*Now* can you tell us?"

"Tell you what?" Jaclyn asked, her face wearing the mask of innocence she normally reserved for Miss Swanson.

"Come on," I said. "You owe it to us."

Jaclyn looked down at me from the top step where she stood. "I don't *owe* you anything," she said. "If anyone owes anything, you owe me."

"But was it you?" Claire asked. "Did you cast a spell on Lela's grandfather?"

Jaclyn considered for a moment. "All I will say is this, don't forget the first rule of the Magic Club." *Everything in the Magic Club is secret.* How could we forget? "And anyone who slips up, anyone who leaks—all I have to say is, watch out."

"What do you mean?" I said.

Jaclyn frowned at me. "Worse things could happen than your grandfather getting sick."

After that, I started having nightmares. In my dreams, aliens were attacking the Earth and taking over people's minds with massive, green power rays. I would wake up crying and be afraid to go back to sleep.

One night before bed, I called up Claire to discuss The Magic Club. I asked her if she thought Jaclyn had made Lela's grandfather so sick. Claire said she didn't think so, but she confided that Jaclyn was starting to make her nervous.

"She's my best friend and everything," Claire whispered, as if someone could overhear her on the telephone, "but I don't really like The Magic Club when we do bad spells. I wish we could stick to good spells."

"Me too!" I said. Then, I got an idea. "What if we got all the other girls to agree to do only good spells and then told Jaclyn what we'd decided?"

"She wouldn't like that," Claire said.

"But if we all agreed, then she'd have to agree, too. Right?"

"Maybe," Claire said. "Maybe."

The next day at Reading, Jaclyn's table was full when I got there, so I had to sit with some boys and Lela. At recess, Jaclyn summoned all the girls into a circle to make an announcement.

"It's come to my attention that some people aren't happy with the way The Magic Club is going," she said. No one replied. "I just want to say," she continued, "that people are free to leave at any time." She looked around the circle but avoided my gaze. "If you don't like The Magic Club or the way it's run, then quit."

Again, no one replied. I tried to catch Claire's eye, but she was staring at Jaclyn.

"Okay, then," Jaclyn said. "Let's play." She whispered something to Claire, who started announcing the groups. Claire called off all the other girls for Jaclyn's group, and then said the second group was me and Lela.

"Don't be stupid," I blurted. "I'm not hanging out with her!"

"Yes, you are," Claire said, turning her back on me.

"You can't tell me what to do," I shouted at her. "I'm a five just like you."

"Actually, you're not," Jaclyn interrupted. "You're a four now."

"What?" I said, dumbfounded. "Why?"

"A six does not explain things to a four," she said, hooking arms with Claire. "And neither does a five."

My nightmares continued. To the point, that one night, I woke up screaming so loud it woke my mom. She came in, sat on the edge of my bed, and asked what was wrong. When I thought of what Jaclyn had done to Lela's grandfather, I started to cry. My mom wasn't the kind of parent who pried, so she hugged me for a long time, and when I'd got to the hiccup stage, she rubbed my back.

"Will something bad happen if you tell me?" she asked.

I nodded.

"Well, what's the worst thing this person could do?"

"Make someone sick—maybe even die!" I wailed.

To my dismay, my mom actually chuckled. "And who has that kind of power?"

"You don't understand," I sniffed. "This person can make people do anything. She can even make herself get hundreds on every math test."

"Studying can do that," my mom said.

"No, but she can do other stuff. She can make people hate you. She can tell you in advance what lunch is going to be."

My mom laughed again. "I can tell you what the lunch will be, too," she said.

"What do you mean?"

"I can look it up on the school's website," she said. "The menu is posted there a week in advance. Anyone can see it."

I began to think that Jaclyn wasn't what she was pretending to be.

The next morning before Reading, I announced that I knew what the lunch would be.

"Really?" Lela said. "How do you know?"

"She doesn't," Jaclyn interrupted. "She's just faking."

"No, I'm not," I said.

"Yes, you are. I'm the only one who knows we're having macaroni and cheese."

"I was going to say that!" I cried. The other girls eyed me uncertainly.

"Sure you were," said Jaclyn. "You've got to do better than that if you ever want to be more than a three."

"I'm a four!" I protested.

"Not anymore," she said.

The next morning at school, Jaclyn came up to me while I was putting my coat in my locker. "Hi, *Spencer*," she said in the sweet, knife-like voice she used to speak to Lela.

"Hi, Jaclyn," I replied, as politely as possible. Jaclyn grabbed my locker door, trapping me between it and her body. She brought her broad, lip-glossed mouth close to my face and looked me in the eyes. "What?" I tried to close my locker, but she wouldn't let me. Instead, she fixed me with her gaze, as if she was trying to cast a spell on my mind.

"You've been having bad dreams, haven't you?" she asked.

I stared into my locker, but didn't answer.

"Haven't you?" Jaclyn brought her face closer to mine and whispered in my ear. "I made you have them. And if you tell anyone—your parents, Miss Swanson, *anyone*—I'll cast a *really* bad spell on you."

"You can't do that," I whispered.

"You'll be a one," she said, "and everyone will have more powers than you. Even Lela."

✿ ✿ ✿

I got to class just as Reading was about to begin. The only available seat was with a whole table full of boys. I sat down anyway, trying to look as though I didn't care. Before class could begin, there was a knock on the door. It was Mr. Kermac, the Admissions Office guy. Standing next to him was a tall, pretty Chinese girl. We often had kids visit us for the day if they were applying to the school for next year. We took turns being buddies to the visitors, and so far all the girls had hosted, except me.

"This is Ji-Li," Mr. Kermac told us. "Please make her feel welcome."

As Miss Swanson helped the girl hang up her coat, Jaclyn made Claire pull up an extra chair at their table.

"Let's see," said Miss Swanson, turning to face us, "Whose turn is it to host?"

I was about to answer, but Jaclyn spoke first. "We've got a seat over here, Miss Swanson."

Our teacher looked confused. "Didn't you host last week?"

"I think I know Ji-Li from camp," Jaclyn said. "Can't I be her buddy? Please, Miss Swanson."

Miss Swanson half-smiled. "Oh, do you know each other already?" she asked our visitor.

"No," Ji-Li said flatly.

"It's my turn," I heard myself say. All the girls looked at me. "Jaclyn went last time."

"But Miss Swanson," Jaclyn persisted, "Spencer's table is full, and we have a chair right here."

Miss Swanson squinted at Jaclyn, then at me. I didn't know why I was standing up to Jaclyn, but I pulled an extra chair next to mine and smiled at the visitor. "You can sit here, Ji-Li," I said, "we're just about to start Reading." Miss Swanson seemed relieved, and Ji-Li sat down next to me. As Claire began reading aloud, though, Jaclyn caught my eye. She held up one finger, and then looked away.

At recess, Jaclyn and Claire got Ji-Li to hang out with them even though they didn't say anything about The Magic Club, and by lunchtime, it was clear that my hosting duties had been hijacked. At the end of the day, Jaclyn even got up to take Ji-Li back to the Admissions Office, as was the practice. I tried to ignore them and focused on organizing my homework.

"Jaclyn," Miss Swanson called out, as they opened the door, "where are you going?"

"I'm just taking Ji-Li downstairs, Miss Swanson."

"Isn't Spencer her host? Spencer can take her."

Jaclyn looked ready to cast her old sweet-as-sugar spell. "But—"

"Have a seat, Jaclyn," Miss Swanson interrupted, sharply. "Spencer will take her."

I got up without looking at Jaclyn and led Ji-Li down the hall. To my surprise, she spoke to me.

"What's with that Jaclyn girl?" she asked. I stopped and stared at her. "I mean, she acts like she runs the whole school."

I looked around to make sure there was no one in the hall. "Yeah," I said.

"Why do you put up with it?"

I took a deep breath. Why did we? Why did I? I couldn't explain it, and if I tried, Jaclyn would find out, and something really bad would happen. Something even worse than being a one.

"You should stand up to people like her," Ji-Li continued. "Otherwise, they turn into monsters."

"You don't understand," I whispered impulsively. "She can cast spells. She made someone's grandfather get really sick."

I expected Ji-Li to laugh, but she didn't. "If she's casting spells, then you need protection."

"What do you mean?"

Ji-Li thought for a moment. "You need something to keep that girl from casting spells on you—like an amulet."

I remembered reading about amulets and how they could protect you from evil magic, but I'd never heard of anyone making them. "How would you do that?" I asked.

Ji-Li shrugged. "I'm not an expert or anything, but it should be something you can wear on your body, like a necklace or a bracelet, and it should have in it something of yours and something of hers—like a hair or something." I nodded. I could do that. I could make that. "Plus," she continued, "since you want to reflect her evil spells back on her, it should have a piece of mirror or something in it. That's all. But I really don't know."

We'd arrived at the Admissions Office. I smiled and on impulse gave Ji-Li a hug. "Thanks," I gushed. "I hope you come here next year."

"I'll think about it," she said, "if you take care of that girl."

That day by the lockers, I plucked one of Jaclyn's hairs without her noticing, and that night I made my amulet. I twisted her hair with one of my own and wrapped them inside a piece of tinfoil. Then, I made designs on the tinfoil and strung it on a piece of leather from an old necklace. I wore it to bed, and for the first time in a long time, I had no nightmares.

The next day at school, I ignored Jaclyn completely. At recess, I took out my bag of tinfoil and started fashioning more charms for my amulet necklace. Later, Lela cornered me in the bathroom to ask what was going on. I explained about my amulet and how it made Jaclyn powerless over me. That night, Lela called me up and asked me to make her an amulet.

By Christmas vacation, every girl in the fourth grade was wearing my amulet necklaces, even girls in the other class who knew nothing about The Magic Club. Jaclyn even made one of her own, but everyone knew it was a fake.

Jaclyn didn't *always* have the best ideas. My amulet idea was pretty good. I think the others thought so, too.

Flying

NELL CROSS

Melanie isn't afraid—of anyone or anything. Not even of flying alone. Boy, does Lily have a lot to learn!

"Sweetheart, it will be over before you know it, I promise." Lily's mom said, wiping the tears from Lily's face. "And then you'll be back home in just two days."

Lily couldn't believe she was standing in the middle of the airport crying like a baby. How embarrassing. She knew it wasn't a big deal to get on the forty-minute flight to visit her dad in San Diego, but it was the first time she was flying by herself. All week, she had been looking forward to the visit, but when it came time to actually say goodbye to her mom, she got a hot lump in her throat.

"Now, remember," Lily's mom continued, "don't talk to strangers. If you need help, ask someone wearing an airline uniform." Lily nodded, knowing this was just the beginning of her mom's list of cautions. "I want you to call me when you land—before you even leave the airport. Here are some quarters to call. Make sure to keep them in a special place in your wallet. And keep your purse zippered and with you at all times—don't leave it at your seat if you go to the bathroom."

"Okay, okay, Mom," Lily said, returning a hug. "Don't worry. I love you."

"I love you too. I can't believe how you're all grown up and flying by yourself," her mom said, squeezing her tight.

A beautiful tall stewardess in a purple uniform walked over and bent down, pinning a pair of small gold plastic wings onto Lily's shirt. "Since this is your first flight alone, you get wings!" the stewardess said brightly. Lily was ashamed that the stewardess could see she was scared, so she gave her a brave smile.

"There you go! Guess what else? You can have all the soda you want!" the stewardess, whose name was Kimberly, said, winking at Lily's mother and leading Lily away.

Lily got to board the plane before everyone else. The stewardess sat her in the window seat of the very first row and helped her buckle her seat belt. She even brought her a plastic cup full of ginger ale to help her get settled in. Lily started to feel silly for getting so upset. It wasn't like this was her first time on a plane, and she always had fun visiting her dad. It just felt weirder than she expected to be traveling alone. She looked out the window and watched the baggage handlers load suitcases into the plane.

"You're in my seat!"

Lily turned with a start. A blond girl was staring at her, and she did not look happy. She was wearing low-cut jeans that flared on the bottom and a black top that said MEL. Lily's mom never let her wear clothing with her name on it, because she thought a kidnapper would be able to call her by name and lure her into his car. Of course, that would never happen in a million years because Lily never would talk to a stranger, even if they *did* know her name.

"1A is always my seat. Kimberly! What's going on here?" The girl's long earrings were swinging with frantic energy.

The stewardess walked over from the tiny kitchen. "Melanie, this is her first flight alone, so why don't you show her the ropes? You can sit in 1B."

"Are you kidding? I don't do middle," Melanie replied.

Kimberly smiled and left to finish her chores. Melanie sat down in 1C, leaving an empty middle seat between her and Lily.

"So you're an U-M?" Melanie asked Lily as she grabbed the extra pillow from the empty seat and put it on her lap.

"A what?" Lily asked.

"A U-M. An unaccompanied minor. You're traveling alone, right? How old are you, ten?"

"I'm eleven."

"Really? Me too! What's your name?"

"Lily."

"I'm Melanie. Welcome to flight 129, service to San Diego!" she said.

"Do you want to sit here? Because I can move," Lily asked.

"Nah. Whatever. I was just giving Kimberly a hard time."

"Do you know her?"

Melanie rolled her eyes. "Duh! I'm on this flight every single weekend, and so is Kimberly. But sometimes this dude named Franz fills in for her. He is lame and a half. He only lets me have one package of peanuts! Like he owns them or something!"

Lily giggled. Kimberly started to recite a speech on the loudspeaker about flight safety. "Please stow away all your personal electronic equipment until the captain informs you of when it is safe to use it. All tray tables must be fully locked and your seat must be in its full upright position." Melanie was mouthing the entire speech word for word. She even knew when to do the hand motions to indicate the emergency exit doors "located forward and aft of the cabin."

"What is aft anyway?" Melanie asked. "If I know the emergency exits are in the aft, but I don't know where the aft is, that doesn't do me much good, now, does it?"

Lily burst out laughing. She had never met anyone her age that was so funny.

The plane rolled over to the runway. They started to go faster and faster, then the wheels lifted up and they were in the air. Lily watched as Los Angeles got smaller and smaller, and soon they were above the wide blue ocean. She felt a hand grab her arm tightly. Melanie was hugging the pillow with her other arm and squeezing her eyes shut.

"Are we above the clouds yet?" Melanie asked, peeking out of one eye.

"Yes," Lily answered.

"Ugh. I hate take-offs. They freak me out. Are your ears

popping? Want some gum?" She popped a stick of Big Red in her mouth, offering one to Lily. They sat for a moment with cinnamon burning their tongues, chomping away.

"So, why are you going to San Diego?" Melanie asked.

"My dad lives there. I'm visiting for the weekend," Lily answered.

"Omigod, mine too! I visit him every weekend. How come I've never seen you on this flight?"

"My mom used to drive me down and my dad used to drive me back, but they got sick of all the driving, and now they think I'm old enough to fly alone," Lily answered.

She had never met anyone else like her who left home and all her friends every single weekend to visit her dad. Her parents had been divorced her whole life, so she wasn't sad that they weren't together, but she did miss out on a lot of stuff her friends did on the weekends.

"Do you have any brothers or sisters?" Melanie asked.

"No," Lily answered.

"Omigod, me either!" Melanie said. Their eyes met and they grinned at each other. Melanie looked down and saw Lily's gold wings pin. "Is that your first one?" she asked. Lily nodded. Melanie reached under her seat and pulled out a big patchwork totebag. "Check it out," she said, showing a solid stripe of gold wing pins circling the top of the bag. "I have enough Frequent Flyer miles to go to China," she said proudly, "First Class!"

While sipping their Cokes and munching on peanuts, Lily and Melanie figured out that they both lived in the same part of Los Angeles, and that neither of their parents had remarried. But unlike Lily's mom, Melanie's mom dated. A lot.

"Her boyfriends are always so lame. Sometimes they try and bring me presents, but they're always, like, for babies. The last one gave me a Wiggles DVD. Can you believe that? I was like, 'Try *Charlie's Angels*, dude!'" Lily giggled while Melanie tossed her hair back. "I'm very old for my years. At least, that's what Kimberly says." Right then, Kimberly walked up with a small metal basket filled with mints.

"Do I have two junior stewardesses on board today?" she asked with a wink.

"Yeah! I'll show Lily," Melanie said, grabbing the basket and whirling around to face Lily. "Kimberly lets me pass out the mints. People are only supposed to take one, but sometimes I let them take two. It's not like I own them or anything!"

The girls started down the aisle, Lily holding out the basket to the passengers on the right side of the plane, Melanie passing it over to people on the left side.

"How are you today, sir? Would you like a refreshing mint?" Melanie asked a man on her side. He was wearing a suit with a bright red tie.

"Thank you. Weren't you on the plane last week?" he asked.

Melanie gave him a big smile. "Yes! You have a good memory. I really like your tie, too."

The man chuckled, "Well, this is my good-luck tie."

"Did it work?" Melanie asked.

"It sure did. You'll now be able to buy Carson's Caramels at all major convenience stores in the greater LA area."

"That's so cool! I love Carson's Caramels. Yum!"

The man beamed, reached down to his briefcase, and pulled out a box of caramels. "Well maybe you would enjoy these, then. I'll trade you for the mint."

"Deal!" Melanie exclaimed, pocketing the candy and passing the mint basket to Lily to offer them to her side of the row. Lily stood in a daze. She couldn't believe what had just happened— Melanie had not only talked to a stranger, but she'd taken candy from him. Lily's mom would have a fit if Lily had done that. But the man seemed really nice. Lily could not believe he would do them any harm.

Melanie talked to a lot of people as they passed the mints. She looked like she was having a lot of fun, too. Lily was way too shy to chat. She could hardly look at the passengers' faces, instead keeping her gaze fixed on the basket of mints.

When they got back to their seats, Melanie offered Lily a caramel.

"Doesn't your mom tell you a gazillion times not to take candy from a stranger?" Lily asked, her mouth watering as Melanie took a bite of a caramel and stretched it from her mouth with her hand.

"Yeah, but, it wasn't like that guy came up to me and was trying to get me alone and eat his candy. He was just being nice. Not all strangers are bad, you know." Melanie got a funny look on her face and started to make choking sounds. Lily grabbed her arm, alarmed.

"Are you okay?" Lily asked, her face twisted with worry.

"I think...poison!" Melanie grabbed her neck and stuck her tongue out, sinking down in her chair. Lily reached up to ring the call button, but Melanie slapped her hand down and sat back up.

"Just kidding! Wow, you're easy," Melanie said, swallowing her caramel. Lily was embarrassed at how gullible she was. She turned her back to Melanie and looked out the window, her face burning.

"Oh, don't be like that. I was just goofing around. Here, why don't you have a caramel? Come on, Lily, live a little!" Melanie prodded. "Hey! I think they help your ears pop." Lily turned to look at Melanie. She had stuck a caramel in each ear and had a ridiculous smile on her face. Lily burst out laughing.

"I'm not eating one that's been in your ear!" she said.

"Of course not. Only the best for my new friend," Melanie said, taking a fresh candy out of the box and handing it to Lily. She popped it in her mouth. It tasted like a normal caramel.

When they landed in San Diego, Lily was sad that she had to leave. "So, you're going back to LA on Sunday, right?" she asked Melanie.

"You'll find me on the 5:40, seat 1A. Bye!" Melanie waved, ran to her find dad.

Lily was happy to see her dad, and had fun with him that weekend going to the beach and riding their bikes. All weekend she thought about Melanie, and wondered what she was doing. Melanie's dad had picked her up in a jeep that didn't have any kind of roof. It looked so fun to ride in. Lily's mom would have said it was too dangerous. She could just hear her voice, "I hope they don't flip over—they'll die immediately." Her mom was always imagining the worst-case scenarios.

Finally, Sunday afternoon rolled around and Lily was at the San Diego airport. Lily looked everywhere for Melanie, but didn't see her. Kimberly told her that she had to board, so she gave her dad a big hug and said goodbye. She immediately got a knot in her stomach like she did saying goodbye to her mom, and felt tears coming to her eyes. She tried to keep on swallowing them down. It was just so hard to say goodbye, and scary to get on the plane alone again. She thought Melanie was going to be there to keep her company. Just to be safe, she sat in 1B.

General boarding started and the plane filled up with passengers. A huge man sat next to Lily, taking 1A—his belly spilled into part of 1B! Lily's heart sank. She picked up the in-flight magazine and started to blankly thumb through it, trying not to cry.

"Excuse me sir, but I would really appreciate if you would let me sit next to my sister."

Lily's head shot up. Melanie!

"There's a perfectly lovely window seat just across the aisle. In fact you might find you have even more legroom!" Melanie went on, batting her large blue eyes at the man. He grunted and lumbered over to the other seat. Melanie plopped down next to Lily just as the pilot announced it was time to get ready for take-off.

"Sister?" Lily giggled, giddy that Melanie had shown up.

"He believed me! We could totally be sisters." Lily looked at Melanie. She had another trendy outfit on, and a cool sparkly rhinestone bracelet with matching earrings dangling from her ears. Lily's mom said she wasn't allowed to get her ears pierced until she turned thirteen. "Whoops, forgot to turn off my cell phone!"

Melanie said as Kimberly announced it on the loudspeaker. Yet another cool thing Melanie had that Lily didn't.

"Maybe we could switch families like they did in that movie about the twin sisters," Lily said.

"But then we couldn't play together because we'd be at each other's houses. I have a better idea—why don't you sleep over tonight!" Melanie said.

Lily flushed with excitement. Even though she had just met her, she really felt like Melanie could be her sister. She just had to figure out how to get her mom to agree. Whenever she had play dates with friends from school (which happened less and less since she was visiting her dad every weekend), her mom had to have the address, phone number, cell phone number, and e-mail of both parents before she could go.

Kimberly let them pass out the mints again. A woman with red hair remembered Lily from Friday's flight. "Looks like we're on the same schedule! Did you have a nice weekend in San Diego?" Lily's heart started to beat quickly. She wanted to say something, but the words got stuck in her throat, so she just nodded and squeezed out a smile, moving on to the next row as quickly as possible. Melanie didn't get nervous talking to anyone, and even talked to this really cute boy playing a Game Boy in the last row. Lily had seen him when they boarded the plane, but would never in a million years have been brave enough to talk to him.

When they got back to their seats, Lily asked, "How do you just talk to people like that?"

"What do you mean?" Melanie asked, confused.

"I don't know, I just get so nervous talking to people I don't know. You seem like you can talk to anyone and you don't get freaked out at all."

Melanie thought for a moment. "Well, you know, the easiest way to talk to someone is to give them a compliment. Most people like that. And then you can just go from there."

Lily nodded. That certainly did seem easy. She vowed to try it soon. But right now, she wanted to focus on getting her mom to let her sleep over at Melanie's.

Fifteen minutes later, their plane landed in LA. Melanie and Lily walked off the plane holding hands to show their moms what good friends they were. While Lily's mom was squishing her in a hug, she saw Melanie's mom kissing Melanie's cheek and straightening her hair. Melanie's mom looked like a fashion model, with a short funky haircut and lots of eye makeup. Her nails shimmered in gold glitter. Lily tried to remember if she'd ever seen her mother wear nail polish in her whole entire life.

"So, is the lovely Lillian going to be camping out with the girls tonight?" Melanie's mom asked.

"Uh, hello, I'm Mrs. Coleman," Lily's mom said extending her hand formally.

"Hey there, I'm Nikki," Melanie's mom said giving a strong handshake. "Sounds like our frequent flyers are new best friends." Melanie grabbed Lily's hands and clasped them in her own, and they started giggling. Lily's mom put her hand on Lily's shoulder, trying to calm her down.

"Yes, they do seem to get along quite well," Lily's mom started, hesitating, "but I'm afraid she has other obligations tonight." She squeezed Lily's shoulder and pulled her closer.

Lily whirled around. "What? I did all my homework at Dad's. Can't I sleep over?"

"I can drive her to school tomorrow," Melanie's mom said encouragingly.

Lily's mom bit her lip, looking anguished. "Maybe next time, but tonight Lily needs to clean up her room." Lily scowled. Her room was clean already. She knew her mom was just making an excuse. Her mom tightened her arm protectively around Lily, giving her a pleading look. Lily wriggled free and stepped away, turning her back on her mother.

Melanie's mom tried to ease the tension, "Maybe you can both come over next week. We can make tacos or something."

Lily took a step closer to her mom. "My mom makes a killer guacamole," she said hopefully.

Lily's mom chewed on her lip. "We'll see," she said with a half smile, "Okay, Lily, let's get going. Say goodbye. It was nice to meet you." She reached out to shake Melanie's mom's hand. Instead, Melanie's mom hugged her.

Melanie squeezed Lily tightly, and they pressed their foreheads together. Melanie slipped off her rhinestone bracelet and put it on Lily's wrist. "You can give it back next week." Lily smiled.

On the way home, Lily and her mom stopped to get gas. Lily's mom got out and put the pump in the car. On the other side of the pump, Lily saw a man pull up with a fluffy Golden Retriever sticking his head out the back window. He was a little clumsy getting out of his car, but he seemed nice, like a librarian. Lily watched as he put the pump in his car and tried to pump the gas, but nothing was happening. Flustered, he got a nervous smile on his face.

"Excuse me," he said to Lily's mom. Her back stiffened and she took a step backward. "I can't seem to figure this out. How do you get the gas to start?"

"You have to pay first. Tell them what number pump you're at." She said it shortly, putting her pump back and replacing the fuel cap on the car. Leaning into Lily's window, she said, "I'm going to go in to get my change. Watch my purse."

"Can I get a slushie?" Lily asked.

"Not before dinner," her mom said, walking away

"Come on Mom, live a little!" she called through the window. Her mom threw a disapproving face over her shoulder.

Lily rolled down her window all the way and leaned out, looking at the dog. The man returned and began to successfully pump gas into his car. Lily took a deep breath, her heart racing, and blurted, "I like your dog."

The man jerked his head up and looked around. He saw Lily and gave a broad smile. "Thanks! Do you have a dog?"

"No. My mom said they would ruin the furniture. What's his

name?" Lily couldn't believe how easy it was to talk to a perfect stranger.

"Bo. Sometimes I call him Bo Bo." Lily could see the dog wagging his tail in the car.

"Lily, who are you talking to?" her mother said sternly as she got back into the car.

"His dog's name is Bo Bo," Lily said, pointing to the man. The man waved to Lily's mom.

"You have a very sweet daughter," the man said.

"Thank you," Lily's mom answered, blushing slightly. "Goodbye!" She pressed the button to roll up Lily's window and started the car. The man waved goodbye and Lily waved back, through the closed window.

"Why were you talking to that man?" Lily's mom asked as they pulled out of the gas station.

"I thought his dog was cute. He was just being nice." She turned to look at her mom. "You know, not *all* strangers are bad."

Her mom scowled defensively and pulled her hair off her face, winding up to start a lecture. But then she studied Lily's earnest face for a moment and sighed. "I suppose you have a point, sweetheart," she smiled at her wearily. "Look in the bag—I got you something." Lily hadn't even noticed that her mom had bought something at the gas station. She opened the bag, expecting to find a bottle of chewable vitamins or something else boring and sensible. It was a box of Carson's Caramels.

"Omigod!" Lily exclaimed.

Her mom smiled and stroked her hair. "I decided to 'Live a little.' They're a new kind of candy the store was promoting."

"I know, Mom," Lily said, leaning over to kiss her on the cheek. "Thanks."

Georgia's Peach

CLAIRE MYSKO

*Georgia's birthmark makes her feel self-conscious and ugly.
That is, until she meets one very unusual puppy.*

G eorgia stared hard at her reflection. It was still there, of course. That pink birthmark right smack in the middle of her left cheek. No amount of wishing would make it disappear. She hated that her face just wouldn't cooperate.

She didn't always have such a terrible relationship with her birthmark. When she was little, it wasn't a problem at all. Her mother used to tuck her in every night with their bedtime ritual.

"Good night, my sweet Georgia."

"Good night, Mom."

"And good night to my sweet Georgia's peach!"

She would kiss her cheek like it was the most special cheek she had ever seen. It was funny then, especially because the birthmark was sort of shaped like a peach. In those days, Georgia would prance around parties showing it off to every guest and relative who would pay attention. According to her mother, she once walked right up to an unsuspecting woman in a grocery store and proclaimed loudly that peaches were the sweetest fruit in the whole wide world. This must have seemed strange, especially since they were standing in the deli line, a solid ten aisles away from anything resembling fruit. She was only four at the time, so Georgia didn't remember much about the incident—except for the scary "stranger danger" lecture she got on the car ride home.

But now she was eleven, and her peach didn't feel so special anymore. Every day at school, she felt her face burning. Most kids tried to look into her eyes when they talked to her, but she could sense them trying not to look, and that only made it worse. She knew that dreadful spot distracted them. After all, it was impossible to miss. She begged her mother to take her to a doctor to get it removed, but she always got the predictable "wait until you're older" response. She was beginning to think that she might die of embarrassment before she even made it to the age of twelve. Georgia squinted. With her eyes half closed, everything blurred together nicely. She almost looked normal.

Her mirror moment was interrupted by the phone ringing.

"Geooorgia!! Elephone-tay or-fay oo-yay!" Tom screamed

from the bottom of the stairs. For a big brother, Tom was seriously lacking in the maturity department. He spent most of his time being a complete goofball. But then again, he had nice clear skin and a mop of curly brown hair that would pretty much guarantee a giggle-fest when he flipped it out of his eyes right after delivering one of his cheesy punchlines. It didn't really matter what came out of his mouth. He had at least three seventh grade admirers who always thought he was sooo hysterically funny. Tom loved the spotlight. Georgia hated it. Her stupid birthmark made it seem like she had her own personal spotlight shining on her 24/7. Most of the time, all she wanted to do was duck into darkness.

"Got it!" Georgia flopped on her bed with the phone to her ear.

"Hey, check this out..." Her BFF, Jasmine, started every conversation with those same four words. "Mr. Connors said he would be a teacher sponsor of an animal rights club!"

"Wow, how did you find out?" Georgia replied.

"Julie has a class with him. She just IM'ed me. And check this out—he said there would be a few spaces for sixth graders."

Georgia was excited, but she didn't want to get her hopes up until she had all the facts. Jasmine had good intentions, but she was widely known as Grovetown Middle's walking, talking tabloid. Her "inside info" was not exactly 100% reliable.

"And you thought of me?" Georgia asked. "Gee, I wonder why!"

"No kidding, Miss Veg-a-licious! You were born to be in that club. Don't know much now, but I'll hit you back with more details. Oops, that's my other line. Gotta go. Bye!"

Georgia hung up the phone with Jasmine feeling like she had just jumped off a merry-go-round that was spinning way too fast. That girl could buzz in and out before you could even process what she had said.

If there were actually an animal rights club in the works, it would be pretty perfect for Georgia. On the other hand, being part of a club meant looking up, climbing out from under the radar. She wasn't sure if she could deal with that. Georgia wasn't friendless by any means, but she was comfortable enough with the friends she had. People like Jasmine had grown up with her, which meant they had grown up with her birthmark, too. They were used to it by now. They could almost look past it. It was different with new people, though. There was this big obstacle to overcome, this blotch of ugliness standing between her and the rest of the world.

She stretched out and caught a glimpse of the footprint on her ceiling. Last summer, her not-so-brilliant cousin Allison saw a spider up there and had the not-so-brilliant idea to throw her shoe at it. Personally, Georgia thought Allison deserved to be squashed more than that spider, and she took great pleasure in knowing that the defenseless insect got away safely, thanks to Allison's terrible aim. The shoeprint remained as a pleasant reminder of the failed assassination attempt. Georgia loved all creatures—creepy, crawly, furry or slimy.

That night, she scooped up her cat Scooby from his regular snoozing spot under the kitchen table.

"You're cuddling with me tonight, kitty." She gave him a squeeze. There was something about his purring that made it easier for Georgia to fall asleep, despite her worries. In the moonlight, she could just make out the rise and fall of his steady breathing. She would find out more about the club tomorrow. And maybe she would find more courage to take a risk and join.

"Hey, check this out!" Jasmine was barreling toward her waving a sheet of green paper. Georgia stacked her math and history books neatly in her locker and placed her lunch bag on top. It was way too early in the morning for Jasmine's spastic energy.

"Okay, let me see." Georgia gave her combination lock a quick spin before she took the paper to inspect it for herself.

"So? What do you think? Are you gonna sign up?" Clearly, Jasmine was not going to let this one go without an answer.

"Yeah, I think so. Will you come with me?"

"I think I can probably go. I just need to check and see if I have to baby-sit. Hey, do you think your mom can be a driver? She'd probably be way into it. Plus, I want to ride in her cute little Volkswagon bus! That thing should be in a museum!"

Jasmine was right. Georgia's mother would love the idea of this club. In fact, Georgia had inherited her love of animals from her mom.

"I'll ask her later. So, you'll go if you can?"

"Yes, silly. Come on, let's add our names to the list!"

Once she had signed her name (in permanent, everlasting, un-erasable ink) to that piece of paper outside of Mr. Connor's office, Georgia was filled with a mixture that was one part excitement and three parts dread. What had she gotten herself into? She spent all of Tuesday and Wednesday imagining the many possible disastrous scenarios that could unfold on this trip. Her mom had agreed to be a driver, so that added even more potential for embarrassment. From the looks of the sign-up sheet, it was mostly seventh and eighth graders going, and Georgia had very little contact with older kids. Besides her brother, of course. She couldn't stand the thought of anyone feeling sorry for her, and that's exactly what she feared would happen. Everyone would be polite, but really they'd be thinking of her as the poor little sixth grader with the big birthmark. She tried hard not to think that way, but it just didn't seem fair.

By the time the final bell rang on Thursday, Georgia was desperate to just get the whole thing over with. She had spent so much energy worrying about it, that she completely dismissed the idea that it might actually be something to look forward to. As she walked out the doors and into the parking lot, she could see a small group gathering. Most of the kids were clustered around the hippie mobile. Her mother was precisely on time, as usual.

"Georgia! Georgia! Over here!" Jasmine was waving frantically. Great, just great. She had planned to stroll up casually, but now everyone had turned around to see who the heck Jasmine was screaming at. She would have to walk across the length of the parking lot with a sea of faces looking straight at her. It was a good thing her birthmark wasn't visible from this distance. At least she could pretend for a second that she was cool and confident. But that would change as she got closer.

"Welcome!" Mr. Connors patted Georgia on the back. "We sure are lucky your mom agreed to be a chauffeur today! However, it seems that everyone wants to go in her cool car, and no one wants to be seen in my boring clunker!" He threw his head back and laughed until a few kids were comfortable enough to join him in a semi-chuckle. Mr. Connors always made corny jokes. And he always laughed at himself. Georgia supposed it was better than having no sense of humor at all.

"Well, according to my handy list here, we're just waiting for a few more. So why don't you chat before departure time?"

Georgia nodded and smiled before she looked around to catch Jasmine's eye. She was so relieved that she wasn't on her own.

"I'm Macy. Macy Brunell." A tall, skinny redhead stepped forward and waved a quick hello. "And this is Joe." She nodded to the boy standing next to her. Georgia learned that Macy was in sixth grade, too, and had recently moved to Grovestown from Los Angeles. Georgia's mom was quick to jump in on that one.

"L.A., really? Ever see any fabulous movie stars?" Georgia groaned and rolled her eyes. But apparently the Volkswagon bus was like her mom's free pass to say whatever she wanted. Everyone laughed at her joke.

Joe was an eighth grader, although Georgia would never have guessed that he was 13. He was much shorter than the other eighth grade boys. Tasha (pronounced "Taahh-sha" for flair) was, too. By the time the stragglers arrived and they were all piling into the cars, Georgia had almost managed to swallow the pit of nerves that had been stuck in her throat.

Carroll Farms Animal Shelter was a completely humane "community," as Amber the Volunteer Relations Coordinator explained while she gave her tour. It did look like a pretty nice place to be a homeless animal. Georgia had never visited an animal shelter before, but she had always imagined rows of tiny cages with sad little cats and dogs inside them. This place, however, was practically a resort, with sprawling green lawns and designer pet toys, and even a pond. She couldn't imagine that any animal would want to leave this place!

"What happens if no one adopts an animal? Do you um... well, you know." Taahh-sha twirled the end of her braid around her finger and cocked her head to one side.

"Oh, we never euthanize. That's one of the most important parts of being a humane community." Amber had definitely heard this question before. "We have a constant flow of volunteers—and I'm hoping some of you might consider being part of that group—

who help to take care of our facilities. Each and every animal is precious to us." There was a collective sigh of relief.

"Oh, no! What happened to that one?!!" Georgia turned to see Jasmine pointing at a puppy being led past the group on a leash.

"Yeah, she's missing a leg. What happened to her?" Joe asked.

The woman leading the dog stopped to chat with the group. Georgia could see that the puppy was missing one of its back legs.

"This is one of our newest residents! And actually, she was born this way. Her brothers and sisters have all been adopted, but, as you can see, she requires a little extra TLC."

Meanwhile, the puppy was jumping playfully and barking. Georgia knelt down to pet her, and the dog's ears perked happily.

"Oh, that is so sad." Jasmine was on the verge of tears. Georgia couldn't help but notice that the puppy looked far from sad. That dog was oblivious to the misfortune that everyone else was focused on. She danced about proudly on those three legs as if she was the most charming puppy that ever lived. And Georgia was beginning to think that she might have the right idea.

"How does she get around with only three legs?" Macy posed the question that everyone seemed to be wondering about.

"Well, seems to me she's getting along just fine!" Mr. Connors patted the puppy on the head and looked to Amber for confirmation.

"Your teacher is right. Most people think this puppy has a big obstacle to overcome, but she runs and plays like all of the other dogs. She wants the same love and attention that any pet wants. Does she look depressed to you?" The puppy gave a little bark, almost on cue.

"Okay, let's get you all back to our offices where you'll watch a short video about our volunteer program."

The woman with the leash said her goodbyes and Georgia watched the dog prance away across the lush green lawn.

On the car ride home, the back of the bus filled with chatter. Macy was already planning for their next project. She thought they should organize a vegetarian bake sale to raise funds for the club. Georgia sat in the front seat, as her mother drove. Usually, she liked that seat, because she could ride facing front, with her back to everyone but the driver (who really should be looking at the road, anyway). But this afternoon, her face wasn't burning with that same awful embarrassment. She hadn't given much thought to looking down or away or anywhere, really. She was mostly thinking about that puppy. Everyone seemed to have noticed the dog for her "imperfection," but Georgia was beginning to see how that one big difference made her even more special. The puppy might not have been aware that there was such a thing as running on four legs, but she had learned how to run on three. And that made her stronger—in more ways than one. Even if the puppy didn't know it, Georgia did.

"So how about it? Are you an official, card-carrying Grovetown Middle Animal Activist now?" her mother joked.

"Definitely. I'm in," Georgia replied. "Hey, do you think you could take me back to see that puppy sometime? Or maybe..."

Her mother stopped at the light before she stole a quick look.

"I think we'll have to talk more, but somehow I have a feeling we'll be seeing a lot more of... Oh, wait. What are we going to name her?"

Georgia smiled to herself.

"How about Peach?"

Author Info

LESLIE MARGOLIS (Spores and Bores) *has written over fifty books for children, under many different names. She's currently working on a young adult novel and a middle grade series. She lives in New York City.*

JESSICA ZIEGLER (Flush It and Forget It) *is a freelance writer in New York City. Zelly, Trish, and Claire all appear in her soon-to-be-finished novel,* Gypsy Chicks. *Jessica is also the Director of Operations at the New York City Department of Homeless Services and holds a Master's Degree in Public Policy from Johns Hopkins University.*

S. K. DUNN (Saga of a Free-Throwing Angel, Fifty Bucks) *wrote her first short story, "Sweetums, the Million-Dollar Sugar Bowl," when she was 9 years old. Currently, she lives in Baltimore, Maryland, where she studied creative writing at Johns Hopkins University. She has taught composition and creative writing to all age groups, from six to sixty. She lives with her dog, Echo, her cat, Pearl, and one very old plant, Harriet.*

LIESE SHERWOOD-FABRE (Skater Girl) *holds a PhD from Indiana University, Bloomington. She currently resides in Dallas, Texas, with her husband and three children—one an avid skateboarder. Her work has appeared in* Lynx Eye, Duck Soup, *and* CCWriters *magazines, and she has received awards from the Southwest Writers Association and the League for Innovation.*

KRISTEN KEMP (Best Friends and Dog Biscuits) *is the author of* The Dating Diaries *and* I Will Survive. *When not writing, she runs a teen 'zine workshop at The New York Public Library. At home, her naughty Chihuahuas, dog-like cat, and tall Swedish boyfriend keep her from getting lonely.*

KATE HILL CANTRILL (Pretty Much Completely) *is a writer living in Austin, Texas. Her story is based on her own experience of changing schools when she was fourteen years old. She can't remember the name of the girl who first said hello to her, but she is thankful for her company through those first difficult days.*

EMILIE LE BEAU (The Truth About the Queen B) *is a journalist living in Chicago.*

HEATHER ST. CLAIR CROSS (The Magic Club) *is working on her second novel. She lives in Brooklyn, New York, with her husband and two dogs.*

NELL CROSS (Flying) *is a freelance writer and TV producer who is currently finishing her first novel. She lives in New York City with her husband and dog, and has 103,591 frequent flier miles.*

CLAIRE MYSKO (Georgia's Peach) *is a writer and an activist. She is the Assistant Director of Communications at Girls Incorporated, an organization that inspires all girls to be strong, smart, and bold. She lives in New York City.*